EinFach
Englisch
Unterrichtsmodell

Harper Lee

To Kill a Mockingbird

Edited by
Wiltrud Frenken, Angela Luz and Brigitte Prischtt

Series Editor:
Hans Kröger

Vorwort

 Einzelarbeit

 Partnerarbeit

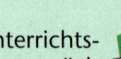 Gruppen-
arbeit

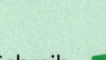 Unterrichts-
gespräch

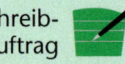 Schreib-
auftrag

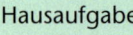 Hausaufgabe

 filmische
Präsentation

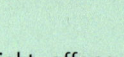 Projekt, offene
Aufgabe

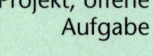 kreative
Aufgabe

 szenisches
Spiel,
Rollenspiel

Der Titel der Reihe **EinFach Englisch** verdeutlicht Zielsetzung und Programm zugleich. Einerseits soll Schülerinnen und Schülern auf einfache Art und Weise der Zugang zu klassischen, aber auch neuen literarischen Werken und Filmen ermöglicht werden, andererseits sollen Lehrerinnen und Lehrern in der Praxis erprobte Unterrichtsmodelle angeboten werden, die die wichtigsten methodisch-didaktischen Ansätze ihres Faches Englisch abdecken. Dabei sind die Modelle direkt, ohne langes Einlesen einsetzbar und stellen Unterrichtsarbeit konkret vor. Als besonders hilfreich für die Praxis haben sich dabei folgende Aspekte erwiesen, die für die Gestaltung der Reihe wesentlich sind:

- Überblick über **Figurenkonstellation**, ggf. **Filmszenen** und **Inhalt**

- **Klausuren** mit **Erwartungshorizont**

- **Arbeitsblätter**, **Tafelbilder** und **Leitfragen** für den Unterricht

- **Piktogramme** als Hinweise auf **Unterrichts-** und **Arbeitsformen**

Das Prinzip der „**Components**" ermöglicht darüber hinaus den variablen Einsatz der Modelle in unterschiedlich konzipierten Unterrichtsreihen. Dabei stehen Machbarkeit und Praxisnähe stets im Vordergrund.

Das vorliegende Modell bezieht sich auf folgende Textausgabe:
Harper Lee: *To Kill a Mockingbird*. New York: Grand Central Publishing 1993,
ISBN 978-0-446-31078-9

Sprachliche Betreuung: Simone Duxbury-Ziemer

© 2009 Bildungshaus Schulbuchverlage
Westermann Schroedel Diesterweg Schöningh Winklers GmbH
Braunschweig, Paderborn, Darmstadt

www.schoeningh-schulbuch.de
Schöningh Verlag, Jühenplatz 1–3, 33098 Paderborn

Druck 5 4 3 2 / Jahr 2017 16 15 14
Die letzte Zahl bezeichnet das Jahr dieses Druckes.

Umschlaggestaltung: Jennifer Kirchhof
Druck und Bindung: westermann druck GmbH, Braunschweig

ISBN 978-3-14-041213-1

Getting started

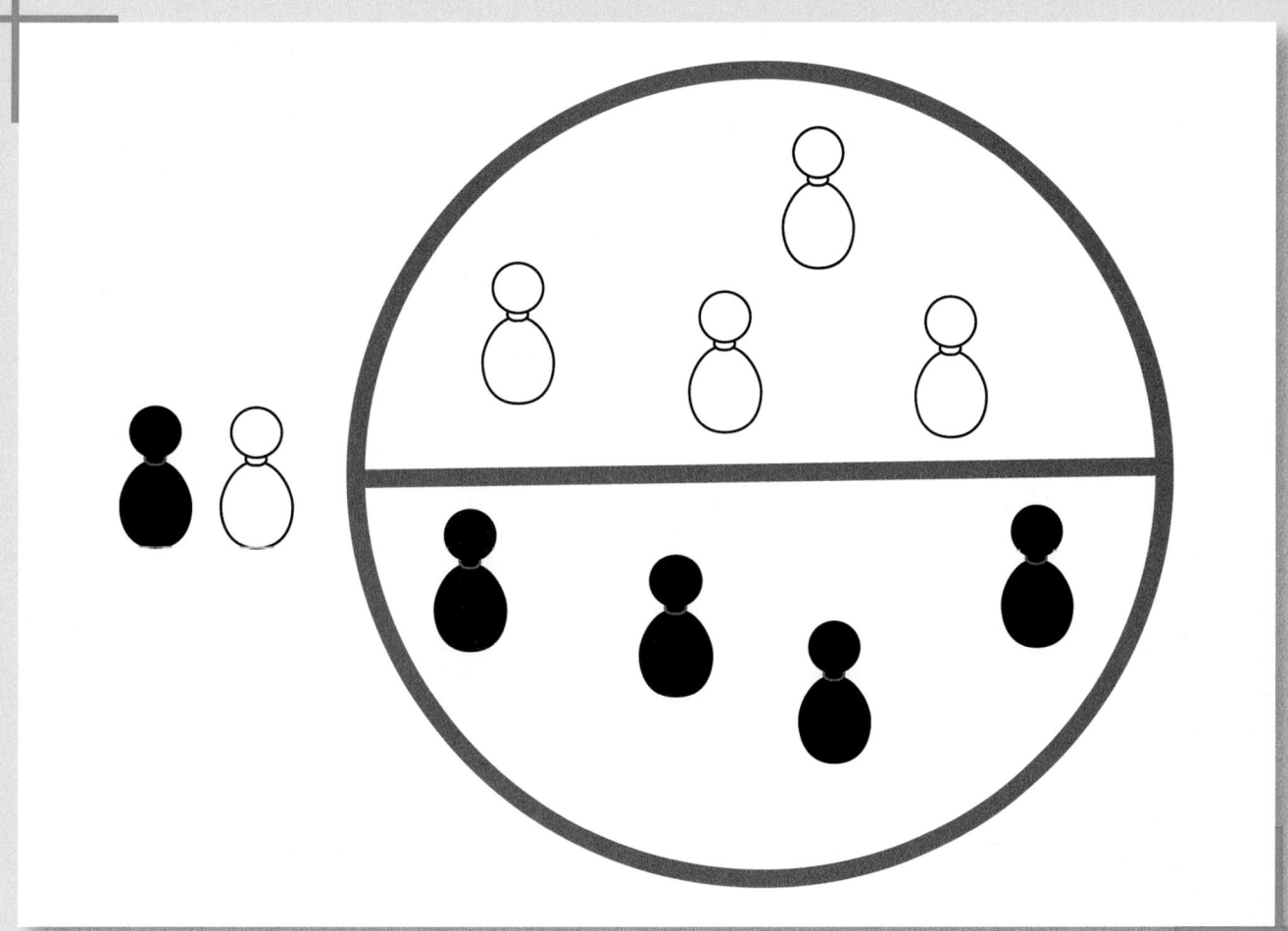

1. Describe the cartoon in detail.

2. Point out the message the cartoonist wants to convey.

3. Find a suitable caption for the cartoon and explain your choice.

Die Personen

Jean Louise (Scout) Finch
Scout ist die Erzählerin des Romans. Sie ist sechs, als die Geschichte beginnt, und neun, als sie endet. Sie ist ein sehr lebhaftes Mädchen, das praktisch nur mit Jungen spielt und sich nicht wie ein braves Mädchen benehmen kann, was ihre Tante Alexandra sehr ärgert. Ihr Vater Atticus Finch bringt ihr bei, die Dinge auch aus der Sicht anderer Leute zu betrachten, was sie auch versucht zu tun. Sie hat einen ausgeprägten Gerechtigkeitssinn. Insgesamt ist sie eine warmherzige, freundliche Person.

Atticus Finch
Atticus, benannt nach dem Römer Atticus, der sich geweigert hatte, im römischen Bürgerkrieg für eine der kämpfenden Seiten Partei zu ergreifen, ist ein allseits respektierter Rechtsanwalt in der kleinen Stadt Maycomb. Er ist ein sanftmütiger Mann, der seine Kinder alleine erzieht, seit seine Frau einige Jahre zuvor gestorben ist.
Obwohl er von Anfang an weiß, dass er nicht gewinnen kann, verteidigt er in einem Prozess den Schwarzen Tom Robinson, der angeblich ein weißes Mädchen vergewaltigt haben soll.

Jem Finch
Jem ist Scouts Bruder, ein zehnjähriger Junge, der am Ende des Romans dreizehn ist. Der Leser sieht, wie er sich von einem Kind, das Spiele spielt, zu einem Teenager entwickelt, der unter Stimmungsschwankungen leidet und das Bedürfnis verspürt, sich von seiner kleinen Schwester und ihren kindischen Plänen zu distanzieren.
Jem hat wie Scout einen ausgeprägten Gerechtigkeitssinn und ist sehr bestürzt über die Vorurteile und die Diskriminierung, die er in Maycomb erfährt. Er möchte wie sein Vater Anwalt werden.

Calpurnia
Calpurnia ist die strenge schwarze Haushälterin des Finch-Haushalts. Sie ist eine der wenigen schwarzen Bewohner von Maycomb, die lesen und schreiben können. Sie tadelt Scout, weil sie zu Walter Cunningham unhöflich ist, aber sie ist auch Scouts liebevolle Freundin, wenn dieser langweilig ist.
Wenn Calpurnia mit ihren schwarzen Freunden zusammen ist, verschweigt sie, dass sie keine Analphabetin ist.

Dill
Dill ist Scouts und Jems Freund, der jeden Sommer seine Tante Rachel besucht. Er ist ein sehr fantasievoller Junge, der sich eine Menge Unsinn ausdenken kann. Es wird deutlich, dass er sehr unglücklich ist, weil er allmählich erkennen muss, dass seine Mutter und sein Stiefvater kein wirkliches Interesse an ihm haben, auch wenn sie ihn mit materiellen Gütern verwöhnen. Dill ist wegen des Ausgangs des Prozesses sehr geschockt.

Tante Alexandra
Tante Alexandra ist die Schwester von Atticus, die voller Vorurteile und Einbildung ist und daher gut zum größten Teil der Bevölkerung Maycombs passt. Sie hat völlig andere Ansichten darüber, wie man ein junges Mädchen erziehen sollte, als Atticus. Obwohl die beiden

in vielen Bereichen unterschiedlicher Meinung sind, zeigt sie Sorge um ihn und die Kinder.

Boo Radley

Boo beschäftigt die Fantasie der Kinder, weil er sich ihnen niemals zeigt und man nur Gerüchte über seine Vergangenheit kennt. Er beschenkt die Kinder, indem er heimlich Spielsachen für sie in einem Baumloch versteckt, bis sein Vater dieses Loch zuzementiert. Offensichtlich nimmt er dennoch weiterhin Anteil am Leben der Kinder, denn er ist es, der am Ende des Romans die Kinder vor dem Angriff von Bob Ewell rettet.

Tom Robinson

Tom ist der Schwarze, der angeblich Mayella Ewell vergewaltigt und misshandelt hat. Er wird trotz offensichtlicher Lügen verurteilt und stirbt, als er kopflos versucht, aus dem Gefängnis auszubrechen.

Bob Ewell

Bob ist der Vater der angeblich vergewaltigten Mayella, der selbst seine Tochter verpügelt hat, als er sah, wie sie einen Schwarzen küsste. Er gehört zur untersten Gesellschaftsschicht in Maycomb, trinkt und lebt in erbärmlichen Verhältnissen. Dennoch gilt sein Wort mehr als das eines schwarzen Mitbürgers.

Der Inhalt

Der Roman *To Kill a Mockingbird* spielt in der fiktiven Kleinstadt Maycomb in Alabama während der Depression in den frühen 30er-Jahren des 20. Jahrhunderts.

Jean Louise „Scout" Finch, die sechsjährige Ich-Erzählerin des Romans, wächst mit ihrem zehnjährigen Bruder Jem bei ihrem alleinerziehenden Vater Atticus auf, der versucht, seinen Kindern die früh verstorbene Mutter zu ersetzen. Bei dieser Aufgabe unterstützt ihn die schwarze Haushälterin Calpurnia. Atticus ist Abgeordneter und Anwalt.

Die beiden Geschwister freunden sich mit Dill an, einem Jungen, der jeden Sommer bei seiner Tante Rachel in der Nachbarschaft der Finchs verbringt.

Der **erste Teil des Romans (Kapitel 1 – 11)** handelt in erster Linie von den Abenteuern der drei Kinder, die versuchen, in Kontakt mit dem geheimnisvollen Boo Radley in ihrer Nachbarschaft zu kommen. Boo wird nie in der Stadt gesehen; er soll von seinem Vater wie ein Gefangener in dessen Haus gehalten werden, weil er als Jugendlicher ein Verbrechen begangen haben soll.

Scout beginnt in diesem Herbst die Schule, ist allerdings enttäuscht, da sie glaubt, dort nichts lernen zu können; sie gerät häufig in Raufereien mit Klassenkameraden.

Der **zweite Teil des Romans (Kapitel 12 – 31)** beschreibt den Prozess, in dem Atticus einen offensichtlich unschuldigen Schwarzen verteidigt, der angeblich ein weißes Mädchen, Mayella Ewell, vergewaltigt und misshandelt haben soll. Obwohl es ganz offensichtlich ist, dass Mayella lügt und von ihrem Vater Bob Ewell geschlagen wurde, weil sie einen Schwarzen geküsst hat, spricht die Jury, die ausschließlich aus Weißen besteht, Tom schuldig und der Richter schickt ihn ins Gefängnis.

Atticus ist sicher, dass er in einem Berufungsverfahren Tom freibekommen wird. Jem ist tief geschockt von dem ungerechten Urteil und kann nicht verstehen, weshalb es nicht zu einem Freispruch gekommen ist. Die meisten Bewohner von Maycomb sind mit dem Urteil aber zufrieden, ihre tief sitzenden Vorurteile sind bestätigt worden.

Tom versucht einige Zeit später seinen Bewachern zu entfliehen und wird auf der Flucht erschossen. Bob Ewell hat geschworen, sich an Atticus zu rächen, weil dieser ihn vor der ganzen Stadt gedemütigt hat. Atticus nimmt diese Drohung nicht ernst. Als Jem und Scout nach einem Historienspiel zu Halloween auf dem Heimweg von Bob Ewell überfallen werden, rettet sie Boo Radley. Bob Ewell bleibt tot zurück.

Der Sheriff Heck Tate besteht darauf, den Tod von Bob als Unfall zu behandeln, um so Gerechtigkeit walten zu lassen.

The author

Nelle Harper Lee was born as the fourth and youngest child of the Lees in Monroeville, Alabama, on April 28, 1926. Her father, a descendant of General Robert E. Lee, was a lawyer, and so she also decided to study law at the University of Alabama, which she did from 1945–49. She also spent a year in England studying at Oxford University. Eventually, however, she gave up her law studies and moved to New York City where she worked as an airline reservations clerk – a career she later gave up in order to work as a full-time writer. In 1957, she sent some short stories to a literary agent, who advised her to revise her material. In that time, her father fell ill and she frequently travelled back to Alabama where her memories of her childhood were refreshed, and thus *To Kill a*

Mockingbird was created and published in 1960. Her childhood friend Truman Capote, a writer himself, became her model for the character named Dill in her novel. She herself was depicted as Scout in her book that is set in fictitious Maycomb, which is modelled on Monroeville, her hometown. From the end of the fifties up to the middle of the sixties, she assisted her friend Capote in writing his best-seller *In Cold Blood* (1966), which is dedicated to her.

After its publication, the novel at once became a best-seller remaining on the bestselling lists for 80 weeks. In 1961, she was awarded the Pulitzer Prize for fiction. A film, starring Gregory Peck as Atticus Finch, was made in 1962 and was also very successful, winning three Oscars.

Suddenly, Harper Lee was a very famous person. Nevertheless, she did not like her popularity as she is basically a very private person. For four decades, she has refused to comment on her novel, preferring it to speak for itself. She has repeatedly told interviewers that she was working on another novel; however, she has never published a second novel.

Nowadays, she lives partly in New York City and partly at her sister's home in Monroeville, Alabama.

Vorüberlegungen zum Einsatz des Romans im Unterricht

Harper Lees Roman *To Kill a Mockingbird* ist seit Jahren ein beliebter Klassiker im Englischunterricht der Sekundarstufe II; ab dem Jahr 2010 z. B. gilt er als Pflichtlektüre für das Zentralabitur in Niedersachsen. Die Beschreibung der Vorgänge in den 30er-Jahren des letzten Jahrhunderts in der fiktiven Kleinstadt Maycomb, im tiefen Süden der USA gelegen, reißt die Schülerinnen und Schüler mit und lädt dazu ein, sich mit den Ungerechtigkeiten, die die Weißen der schwarzen Bevölkerung gegenüber verüben, intensiv auseinanderzusetzen. Thematisch kann man den Roman in die Themenfelder *racism, minorities* oder *discrimination and social injustice* einordnen.

Dabei beschränkt sich der Roman keineswegs auf die Problematik des Zusammenlebens der beiden Rassen, sondern Harper Lee schafft einen Mikrokosmos, in dem verschiedenste Außenseiter ihren Platz finden. So gibt es die chronisch kranke Miss Dubois, den geistig behinderten bzw. verwirrten Boo Radley oder die asozialen Weißen wie die Ewells. Auch die Rolle der Frauen in dieser Gesellschaft und ihre Bereitschaft, sich den Regeln zu unterwerfen, ist ein Thema dieses Romans. Calpurnia als schwarzes Dienstmädchen verschweigt ihrer Gemeinde, dass sie lesen und schreiben kann, Miss Maudie zeigt sich bei der Teeparty bei Aunt Alexandra kämpferisch.

Der Roman kann in drei große Abschnitte eingeteilt werden. Der erste Teil beschreibt die Abenteuer der Kinder, die als Mutproben versuchen, Boo Radley aus dem Haus zu locken. Die zwei folgenden Teile beschreiben die Abenteuer der Erwachsenen, deren Aufmerksamkeit durch den Vergewaltigungsprozess gegen Tom Robinson, einen schwarzen Arbeiter, gefesselt wird. Die Ereignisse, die vor der Urteilsverkündung stattfinden, sind geprägt von Bedrohungen gegen Atticus. Die Ereignisse nach der Urteilsverkündung zeigen den Frust von Jem und einigen anderen Bewohnern, die erkennen müssen, dass es Gerechtigkeit für alle Bewohner in Maycomb noch lange nicht geben wird.

Das Unterrichtsmodell ist so angelegt, dass diese Abschnitte von den Schülerinnen und Schülern vorab gelesen werden. Die Lesearbeit wird motivierend unterstützt durch die entsprechenden **Copies** mit *while-reading*-Aufgaben zum Inhalt sowie zur Wortschatzarbeit.

Die Erzählperspektive trägt eindeutig zum Unterhaltungswert des Romans bei. Er wird von einer Erwachsenen erzählt, die sich an ihre Kindheit erinnert, also vermeintlich aus Sicht eines Kindes. Da diese Sicht jedoch mit den Kommentaren einer Erwachsenen versehen wird, führt dies oft zu Situationskomik.

Erfreulicherweise liegt eine hervorragende Verfilmung des Romans vor, die in diesem Unterrichtsmodell an zwei Stellen zum Einsatz kommt. Es ist auf jeden Fall lohnend, nach der Lektüre den Schülerinnen und Schülern den gesamten Film vorzuführen (*To Kill a Mockingbird,* Robert Mulligan, USA 1962). Gregory Peck wurde für seine Darstellung des Atticus Finch mit dem Oscar als bester Hauptdarsteller ausgezeichnet, außerdem bekam der Film zwei weitere Oscars (Best Art Direction, Best Writing Adapted Screenplay).

Da die zugrunde liegende Ausgabe keine Zeilenzählung aufweist, lässt man in der ersten Stunde von den Schülerinnen und Schülern einen Zeilenmesser aus festem Papier oder Pappkarton anfertigen. Dazu wird ein Streifen Papier so zurechtgeschnitten, dass er wie ein Lesezeichen in das Buch gelegt werden kann. Auf diesem Streifen trägt man dann die Zeilenzahlen ein und kann ihn so für jede Seite verwenden, um auf einen Blick die Zeilenzahlen von Zitaten angeben zu können.

Die Seitenangaben im Modell beziehen sich auf folgende Ausgabe: Harper Lee, *To Kill a Mockingbird,* Grand Central Publishing, New York, 1993.

Klausuren

Im Folgenden werden zwei Klausurvorschläge zum Roman *To Kill a Mockingbird* vorgestellt.

Klausur 1 ist eine literarische Textaufgabe. Der zugrunde liegende Text ist ein Textauszug aus dem Roman. In der Klausur sollen die von einzelnen Damen bei einer Teegesellschaft im Hause Finch geäußerten Vorurteile gegenüber der schwarzen Bevölkerung herausgearbeitet werden. Diese Klausur empfiehlt sich nach der Lektüre des gesamten Romans, da die Schülerinnen und Schüler mit allen im Roman geschilderten Vorgängen vertraut sein müssen. Der Textauszug hat einen Umfang von 665 Wörtern, ist daher gut für einen Grundkurs, aber auch für einen Leistungskurs geeignet.

Klausur 2 ist aufgrund seiner Länge (757 Wörter) eher für einen Leistungskurs geeignet, könnte aber für einen Grundkurs gekürzt werden.
Der zugrunde liegende Text ist eine Rede des damaligen Senators (heute US-Präsident) Barack Obama über die immer noch zu beklagende Benachteiligung der afro-amerikanischen Bevölkerung. Er führt die missliche Situation vieler schwarzer US-Bürger auf Fehler in der Geschichte zurück und stellt einen Wandel in Aussicht. Somit bietet es sich an, diese Klausur frühestens nach Bearbeitung von *Component 2* zu stellen, da die Schüler über grundlegendes Hintergrundwissen zur Diskriminierung der Afro-Amerikaner verfügen sollten.

Excerpt from *To Kill a Mockingbird* (chapter 24)

"[…] J. Grimes Everett said to me, he said, 'Mrs Merriweather, you have no conception, no conception of what we are fighting over there.' That's what he said to me."

"Yes ma'am."

"I said to him, 'Mr Everett,' I said, 'the ladies of the Maycomb Alabama Methodist
5 Episcopal Church South are behind you one hundred percent.' That's what I said to him. And you know, right then and there I made a pledge in my heart. I said to myself, when I go home I'm going to give a course on the Mrunas and bring J. Grimes Everett's message to Maycomb and that's just what I'm doing."

"Yes ma'am."

10 When Mrs Merriweather shook her head, her black curls jiggled. "Jean Louise," she said, "you are a fortunate girl. You live in a Christian home with Christian folks in a Christian town. Out there in J. Grimes Everett's land there's nothing, but sin and squalor."

"Yes ma'am."

"Sin and squalor – what was that, Gertrude?" Mrs Merriweather turned on her chimes
15 for the lady sitting beside her. "Oh that. Well, I always say forgive and forget, forgive and forget. Thing that church ought to do is help her lead a Christian life for those children from here on out. Some of the men ought to go out there and tell that preacher to encourage her."

"Excuse me, Mrs Merriweather," I interrupted, "are you all talking about Mayella
20 Ewell?"

"May –? No, child. That darky's wife. Tom's wife, Tom –"

"Robinson, ma'am."

Mrs Merriweather turned back to her neighbor. "There's one thing I truly believe, Gertrude," she continued, "but some people just don't see it my way. If we just let them
25 know we forgive 'em, that we've forgotten it, then this whole thing'll blow over."

[…]

Mrs Farrow was a splendidly built woman with pale eyes and narrow feet. She had a fresh permanent wave, and her hair was a mass of tight gray ringlets. She was the second most devout lady in Maycomb. She had a curious habit of prefacing everything she said
30 with a soft sibilant sound.

"S-s–s Grace," she said, "it's just like I was telling Brother Hutson the other day. 'S-s-s Brother Hutson,' I said, 'looks like we're fighting a losing battle, a losing battle.' I said, 'S-s-s it doesn't matter to 'em one bit. We can educate 'em till we're blue in the face, we can try till we drop to make Christians out of 'em, but there's no lady safe in her bed
35 these nights.' He said to me, 'Mrs Farrow, I don't know what we're coming to down here.' S-s-s I told him that was certainly a fact."

Mrs Merriweather nodded wisely. Her voice soared over the clink of coffee cups and the soft bovine sounds of the ladies munching their dainties. "Gertrude," she said, "I tell you there are some good but misguided people in this town. Good, but misguided. Folks
40 in this town who think they're doing right, I mean. Now far be it from me to say who, but some of 'em in this town thought they were doing the right thing a while back, but all they did was stir 'em up. That's all they did. Might've looked like the right thing to do at the time, I'm sure I don't know, I'm not read in that field, but sulky … dissatisfied … I tell you if my Sophy'd kept it up another day I'd have let her go. It's never entered
45 that wool of hers that the only reason I keep her is because this depression's on and she needs her dollar and a quarter every week she can get it."

"His food doesn't stick going down, does it?"

conception notion, idea

pledge a solemn promise

to jiggle to move up and down or to and fro with short, quick jerks
squalor filth and misery

to blow over to pass away, to subside

sibilant characterized by a hissing sound

bovine oxlike, cowlike

sulky gloomy, dull

Miss Maudie said it. Two tight lines had appeared at the corners of her mouth. She had been sitting silently beside me, her coffee cup balanced on one knee. I had lost the
50 thread of conversation long ago, when they quit talking about Tom Robinson's wife, and had contented myself with thinking of Finch's Landing and the river. Aunt Alexandra had got it backwards: the business part of the meeting was blood-curdling, the social hour was dreary.

 "Maudie, I'm sure I don't know what you mean," said Mrs Merriweather.
55 "I'm sure you do," Miss Maudie said shortly.

blood-curdling horrifying
dreary causing sadness or gloom, boring

(665 words)

from: Harper Lee: *To Kill a Mockingbird*, New York, Grand Central Publishing 1993, pp. 309–312

Assignments

1. What does the reader get to know about Mrs Merriweather's attitude towards Blacks?

2. Point out the various kinds of prejudices the ladies express and contrast them with Miss Maudie's remark about Atticus.

3. a) The present situation in the USA regarding the position of the Black Americans has certainly changed compared with the era of the thirties. Voice your opinion about the situation of the Blacks in the USA nowadays taking into consideration their fights for equal civil rights.

 b) Miss Maudie writes in her diary about the events of the afternoon, and of course, clearly expresses her opinion about people like Mrs Merriweather. Try to make the diary entry sound emotional and committed.

Erwartungshorizont zu Klausur 1

zu 1: Mrs Merriweather's attitude towards Blacks can be considered as ambiguous: On the one hand, she commits herself to bringing Mr Everett's message to Maycomb (l. 4 – l. 8). On the other hand, she shows various prejudices and even contempt for the black people in her environment. For example:

- Tom Robinson's wife will need some support to lead a Christian life after Tom's death (l. 15 – l. 18);
- she refers to Tom as a "darky", which can be considered as a derogatory term (l. 21);
- she suggests forgiving the Robinson family for what happened although it could clearly be shown that Tom was innocent (ll. 24f.);
- she refers to some people in Maycomb who in her eyes stirred up the Blacks, e.g. supported Tom when he was accused, and who were wrong in her view (l. 40 – l. 43);
- she takes on a patronizing and even scornful attitude towards her maid (l. 44 – l. 46);
- she refers to the maid's head as "that wool of hers" (l. 45).

zu 2: Mrs Merriweather, who covers most of the conversation in this passage, obviously shows a variety of prejudices. For example:

- she maintains that all Blacks need to follow the Christian education and beliefs that she considers to be the true path for herself, and thus not allowing for any other religion or development;
- she still looks at the Robinson family as being "guilty" although Tom's innocence was proven, thereby joining the Maycomb league of racists that uncritically believe in a Black's guilt if accused by a white person (l. 23 – l. 25);
- she refers to the people in Maycomb who supported Tom as being "misguided" just because they supported a Black and does not want to know about their motives; in this way, she is also accusing Atticus (l. 38 – l. 42);
- she considers keeping a maid as an act of charity but in reality looks down on her and does not treat her as an equal person (l. 44 – l. 46).

Mrs Farrow also displays severe prejudices by saying that all the efforts to educate the Blacks as true Christians are futile because as a lady one would be in constant danger of being assaulted (l. 31 – l. 36).

Miss Maudie's remark: "His food doesn't stick going down, does it?" (l. 47) clearly refers to Atticus in whose house the ladies are presenting themselves and their prejudices and whose food they are eating. This sharp remark lets the ladies know that they are voicing opinions which are quite in contrast to what Atticus thinks about the Blacks and what he did for Tom Robinson. Atticus represents just the contrary of what Mrs Merriweather and Mrs Farrow embody. He stands for tolerance towards everybody no matter which colour and believes in reflecting on the reasons why people acted the way they did.

Miss Maudie also represents this liberal attitude and therefore defends Atticus.

zu 3: a) The students could first refer to the fights of the Blacks to have the same rights as the Whites, for example, the peaceful approach (M. L. King) and the more violent supporters (Malcolm X) in the sixties. They could then state some of the goals of the fighters for civil rights and compare them with the present situation. It could be mentioned that:

- a lot of Black Americans still live in poverty or in economically difficult situations;

- there is an unequal proportion of Blacks and Whites in highly-paid jobs;
- many Blacks still live in ghettos;
- despite the busing-system in some areas, there is no real mixing between black and white students in schools;
- when Hurricane "Katrina" hit New Orleans in 2005 and many black people lost everything in the ensuing flooding, the government did not react immediately as it might have done if affluent Whites had been hit.

On the other hand:

- Barack Obama and Jesse Jackson are black candidates who ran for President in 1988 and 2008 respectively; Barack Obama is now the first black President in the US; Condoleezza Rice and Colin Powell were Black Americans in politically high-ranking positions (Defense Secretary; Secretary ot State);
- there has been a lot of affirmative action in order to support Black Americans;
- there are many Black Americans who have played or play an important role in literature (Maya Angelou, Langston Hughes, etc.) or music (Louis Armstrong, Miles Davies, etc.) or the movies/television (Will Smith, Sidney Poitier, Oprah Winfrey, etc.).

zu 3: b) Students should, of course, write from Miss Maudie's point of view, clearly expressing her disdain for the racist and prejudiced attitude of people like Mrs Merriweather and Mrs Farrow. For instance, they could refer to some of the aspects analysed in the second assignment, thereby exposing the ladies as racist and hypocritical. Students could also point out Miss Maudie's anger at the discrepancy between Mrs Merriweather's caring and sympathetic attitude towards the Mruna tribe and her obviously arrogant attitude towards the Blacks in her own environment. Another aspect that could be mentioned is Miss Maudie's appropriately placed sharp remark about Atticus's food with which she set the cat among the pigeons. Students could elaborate on Miss Maudie's reflections before she made this remark and what exactly she wanted to express by it.

Concerning the diction of the diary entry, students should use an emotional and committed style that reflects Miss Maudie's inner state.

Speech by Senator Barack Obama:
A more perfect union

Philadelphia, PA
March 18, 2008

[…]
This was one of the tasks we set forth at the beginning of this campaign – to continue the long march of those who came before us, a march for a more just, more equal, more free, more caring and more prosperous America. I chose to run for the presidency at
5 this moment in history because I believe deeply that we cannot solve the challenges of our time unless we solve them together – unless we perfect our union by understanding that we may have different stories, but we hold common hopes; that we may not look the same and we may not have come from the same place, but we all want to move in the same direction – towards a better future for our children and our grandchildren.

10 This belief comes from my unyielding faith in the decency and generosity of the American people. But it also comes from my own American story.

I am the son of a black man from Kenya and a white woman from Kansas. I was raised with the help of a white grandfather who survived a Depression to serve in Patton's Army during World War II and a white grandmother who worked on a bomber assem-
15 bly line at Fort Leavenworth while he was overseas. I've gone to some of the best schools in America and lived in one of the world's poorest nations. I am married to a Black American who carries within her the blood of slaves and slaveowners – an inheritance we pass on to our two precious daughters. I have brothers, sisters, nieces, nephews, uncles and cousins, of every race and every hue, scattered across three continents, and
20 for as long as I live, I will never forget that in no other country on Earth is my story even possible.

It's a story that hasn't made me the most conventional candidate. But it is a story that has seared into my genetic makeup the idea that this nation is more than the sum of its parts – that out of many, we are truly one.
25 […]

The fact is that the comments that have been made and the issues that have surfaced over the last few weeks reflect the complexities of race in this country that we've never really worked through – a part of our union that we have yet to perfect. And if we walk away now, if we simply retreat into our respective corners, we will never be
30 able to come together and solve challenges like health care, or education, or the need to find good jobs for every American.

Understanding this reality requires a reminder of how we arrived at this point. As William Faulkner once wrote, "The past isn't dead and buried. In fact, it isn't even past." We do not need to recite here the history of racial injustice in this country. But we do
35 need to remind ourselves that so many of the disparities that exist in the African-American community today can be directly traced to inequalities passed on from an earlier generation that suffered under the brutal legacy of slavery and Jim Crow.

Segregated schools were, and are, inferior schools; we still haven't fixed them, fifty years after *Brown v. Board of Education,* and the inferior education they provided, then and
40 now, helps explain the pervasive achievement gap between today's black and white students.

Depression the severe economic problems that followed the Wall Street Crash of 1929. In the early 1930s, many banks and businesses failed, and millions of people lost their jobs in the US and in the UK and the rest of Europe.

William Faulkner (1897–1962) a US writer of novels about the South. He won the Nobel Prize for Literature in 1949.
Jim Crow a system of laws and practices in the US that separated black and white people in the past
Brown v. Board of Education a US legal case which resulted in a famous decision by the US Supreme Court in 1954. It was decided that black students should be allowed to attend the same schools and universities as white students, and this officially ended segregation in the US education system.

16

Legalized discrimination – where Blacks were prevented, often through violence, from owning property, or loans were not granted to African-American business owners, or black homeowners could not access FHA mortgages, or Blacks were excluded from
45 unions, or the police force, or fire departments – meant that black families could not amass any meaningful wealth to bequeath to future generations. That history helps explain the wealth and income gap between black and white, and the concentrated pockets of poverty that persists in so many of today's urban and rural communities.

A lack of economic opportunity among black men, and the shame and frustration that
50 came from not being able to provide for one's family, contributed to the erosion of black families – a problem that welfare policies for many years may have worsened. And the lack of basic services in so many urban black neighborhoods – parks for kids to play in, police walking the beat, regular garbage pick-up and building code enforcement – all helped create a cycle of violence, blight and neglect that continue to haunt
55 us.
[…]

(757 words)

FHA The Federal Housing Administration is a United States government agency. The goals of this organization are: to improve housing standards and conditions; to provide an adequate home financing system through insurance of mortage loans; and to stabilize the mortgage market.

http://my.barackobama.com/page/content/hisownwords

Assignments

1. Point out the reasons why, according to Barack Obama, the USA must become "a more perfect union."

2. Analyse how Barack Obama tries to convince his audience that he will be an extraordinary president by examining the stylistic devices and other techniques of persuasion as well as the content of his speech.

3. Choose one of the following assignments:
   a) Comment on Barack Obama's statement that there is "a wealth and income gap between black and white." (l. 47).

   Or:

   b) Imagine you are a young black American man/woman who finished college two years ago, but still cannot find a well-paid job corresponding to your studies. You have just listened to Barack Obama's speech. Write down your thoughts and feelings about it in a diary entry.

Erwartungshorizont zu Klausur 2

zu 1: The speech *A more perfect union* given by senator Barack Obama in March 2008 deals with the state of race relations in the United States today. He voices the opinion that the inequalities of the past (slavery, Jim Crow laws) have caused problems of disparities between black and white Americans that need to be solved to create a better future for America, a perfect union ("more just, more equal, more free, more caring, more prosperous", ll. 3 f.). Barack Obama states that Black Americans are still disadvantaged by (legal) discrimination and prejudice which prevent them from a good education, a well-paid job and wealth. The resulting lack of economic opportunity leads to a wealth and income gap between black and white people causing shame and frustration in black families.

zu 2: Barack Obama uses numerous means to make his speech convincing. The most important are the following:

line	text	device	function, effect
3	"the long march"	historical allusion	to remind the audience of Martin Luther King's fight for civil rights
3 f.	"more just, more equal, more …"	repetition, enumeration	to point out his main theme and to make the audience remember key-words
5, 6, 7, 18 etc.	"we cannot solve …"	Use of the pronoun "we"	to create identification and solidarity; to emphasize that they are one people and must work together
11 – 21	"my own American story"	personal narrative	to connect with the audience and to create a feeling of familiarity
24	"out of many, we are truly one"	allusion, reference	to remind them of the concept of the melting pot (part of the American dream); "e pluribus unum"
28 f.	"if we walk away now …, we will never be able to …"	metaphor, use of future tense	to create a picture that expresses the urgent need to work together
32	"this reality requires a reminder"	alliteration	to underline the impact of the events that have led to the problems to be solved
33	"The past isn't dead and buried. In fact, it isn't even past."	quotation	to express the idea that racial injustice in the USA still exists
38 f.	"inferior"	repetition	to stress the inferiority of black education
42	„legalized discrimination"	contradiction	to emphasize the injustice black people have had to suffer
43 – 45	"… or … or … or … or … or …	enumeration, anaphora	to intensify his criticism of legal discriminatian
46	"history helps"	personification	to express that people are responsible for the problems of the past and today

zu 3: a) Der Kommentar hängt inhaltlich stark davon ab, welche Themen zuvor im Unterricht besprochen wurden. Beispielsweise können Bezüge hergestellt werden zu Lektüren wie *A Raisin in the Sun.*
The students will probably briefly explain that the reasons for the "wealth and income gap" are to be found in the inequalities of the (distant and more recent) past as well as in the policies of today. They can contrast this reality to various aspects of the American Dream, referring also to the basic ideas of the Declaration of Independence and the American Constitution. The conclusion could describe hopes for a better future.

zu 3: b) Auch der Tagebucheintrag hängt inhaltlich stark von den Themen ab, die zuvor im Unterricht diskutiert wurden, und wird individuell sehr unterschiedlich ausfallen. Grob zu erwarten ist jedoch, dass Obama Zustimmung für seine Darstellung der Situation der afro-amerikanischen Bevölkerung erhält und die Hofffnung geäußert wird, er werde den Afro-Amerikanern zu mehr Chancengleichheit und einem besseren Leben verhelfen. Der Schüler äußert seine Empörung/Enttäuschung über die mangelnden Chancen, trotz Collegeabschluss eine gute Arbeit zu finden, und verweist auf Ungerechtigkeiten, aber auch Errungenschaften in Vergangenheit und Gegenwart. Es könnten auch Vergleiche gezogen werden zwischen den Wahlversprechungen der Demokraten und der Republikaner. Kommentare zu verschiedenen Aspekten des *American Dream* sind ebenso möglich.

Konzeption des Unterrichtsmodells

Am Beginn der ersten drei *Components* steht jeweils die Beschäftigung mit Fragen zum Inhalt des Romanteils, der besprochen wird, und eine *Copy* mit Aufgaben zum Vokabular, das die Schülerinnen und Schüler in ihren aktiven Wortschatz aufnehmen sollten.

In **Component 1** wird als Einführung der Begriff des *outsider* mithilfe einer *mind map* eingegrenzt, um einen Einstieg in die Thematik zu gewinnen. Anschließend liegt der Schwerpunkt auf dem Themengebiet der Charakterisierung, die ausführlich durch Erarbeitung der Unterschiede zwischen *telling* und *showing* und durch weitere wichtige Aspekte auf *Copy 3* behandelt wird. Es wird die Organisationsform eines *character file* dargestellt, die man nun auf verschiedene Figuren des Romans, hier zum Beispiel Scout, anwenden kann. Am Ende des ersten Teils dieses *Components* wird eine ausgearbeitete Charakterisierung von Scout vorgestellt.

Im zweiten Teil des *Component* beschäftigen sich die Schülerinnen und Schüler mit der Ära der *Great Depression* in den USA in den Dreißigerjahren des 20. Jahrhunderts, in deren Folge der sogenannte *New Deal* von Präsident F. D. Roosevelt eingeführt wurde. Diese Epoche bildet den geschichtlichen Hintergrund des Romans. Gleichzeitig werden auch aufgrund der aktuellen Bankenkrise gegenwärtige Entwicklungen anhand von Zeitungsartikeln mit einbezogen. Nachdem eine Passage des Romans auf Hinweise zur *Great Depression* untersucht wurde, geht es anschließend mit einer Bildinterpretation von typischen Bildern aus dieser Zeit weiter. Diese Aufgabe wird durch eine entsprechende *Copy* mit Erläuterungen zur Bildinterpretation unterstützt. Um den Schülerinnen und Schülern einen vollständigeren Hintergrund dieser Epoche zu liefern, wird eine *Copy* als *fact file* zur *Great Depression* bearbeitet.

Zum Abschluss dieses Teils werden zwei Zeitungsartikel aus jeweils den Dreißigerjahren und der Gegenwart, die den Absturz der Börse und seine Folgen thematisieren, sprachlich und stilistisch analysiert. Durch eine Diskussion über Hintergründe und Wirkungsweisen der Finanzkrisen in den Dreißigerjahren und heute wird dieser *Component* abgeschlossen.

In **Component 2** werden die Kapitel 12 bis 19 des Romans erarbeitet. Der Schwerpunkt liegt zunächst auf der Untersuchung der Erzählperspektive, wobei sich die Gelegenheit bietet, die unterschiedlichen in der Literatur verwendeten *points of view* auch allgemein zu wiederholen (*Copies 11 – 13*) und anzuwenden. Dann erkunden die Schüler, wie sich verschiedene Formen von Rassismus in *To Kill a Mockingbird* manifestieren. Den Abschluss dieses *Components* bildet die Analyse einer spannenden Filmszene, in der ein Lynchmob Atticus auffordert, den inhaftierten Tom Robinson herauszugeben. Dabei werden die inhaltliche Struktur der Szene aufgedeckt, filmische Mittel des Spannungsaufbaus sowie der nonverbalen Kommunikation untersucht und die Bildkomposition eines *stills* beleuchtet.

In **Component 3** beschäftigen sich die Schülerinnen und Schüler zunächst mit dem Gerichtsverfahren und Atticus' Rolle als Verteidiger eines Schwarzen. Atticus' Plädoyer wird sprachlich analysiert, und anschließend wird die entsprechende Szene in der Filmversion angeschaut. Im Anschluss daran wird untersucht, wie die Bewohner der Kleinstadt Maycomb auf das Gerichtsurteil reagieren. Ein Rollenspiel rundet diese Arbeit ab, bei dem ein Reporter einer nationalen Zeitung einen der Bewohner für einen Artikel interviewt.

Als weiterer Aspekt wird untersucht, welche Grundsätze zur Erziehung einer „höheren Tochter" in den 1930er-Jahren galten und inwieweit Scout einer solchen Erziehung gerecht wird.

Dabei wird der stereotype Begriff der *Southern Belle* untersucht. Eine Charakterisierung mit wenigen Adjektiven schließt diesen Teil der Romanbesprechung ab.

Als Abschluss der Behandlung des Romans bietet sich eine Runde *Touch, turn, talk* an, die alles Wissen der Schülerinnen und Schüler über den Roman in einem Abschlussgespräch aktiviert.

Component 4 bietet eine ganze Reihe von Zusatzmaterialien an, die im Anschluss an die Besprechung des Romans oder während der Lektüre als Hintergrundinformation angeboten werden können. Zunächst findet sich eine Aufgabe, die mithilfe des Internets in Einzel- oder Gruppenarbeit gelöst werden kann. Der Kurs soll eine *timeline* der Bürgerrechtsbewegung in den USA erstellen.

Nach dieser historischen Einordnung der Geschehnisse in Maycomb werden weitere Texte vorgestellt. Zunächst geht es um einen ähnlich ungerecht verhandelten Gerichtsfall, den Prozess gegen die neun Scottsboro Boys, die wie Tom Robinson fälschlich angeklagt waren, ein weißes Mädchen vergewaltigt zu haben. Danach wird Material zu Billie Holidays bekanntem Song *Strange Fruit* geboten, durch den die Sängerin weltberühmt wurde. Der Text wurde von einem Lehrer geschrieben, der von der Fotografie eines gelynchten Schwarzen tief beeindruckt war. Ein Auszug aus Joyce Carol Oates Roman *Black Girl/White Girl* rundet die Behandlung dieses Themas ab.

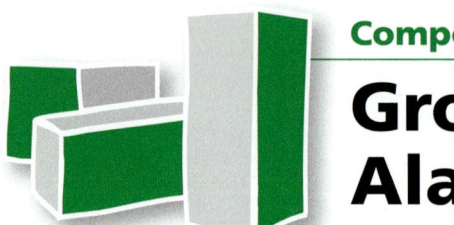

Growing up in Southern Alabama

1.1 It takes a village to raise a child

Der erste *Component* beschäftigt sich mit der Erarbeitung der Kapitel 1–11 des Romans, in denen Atticus, Scout und Jem in ihrem geordneten Leben in der Kleinstadt Maycomb vorgestellt werden, welches trotz der aufziehenden *Great Depression* anfangs ruhig und gleichmäßig verläuft, nur unterbrochen durch Ereignisse wie z. B. das Erforschen des geheimnisumwobenen Radley-Hauses oder das Abbrennen von Miss Maudies Haus. Im weiteren Verlauf des Romans entwickeln sich größere Turbulenzen durch die Ereignisse im Zusammenhang mit dem Vorwurf, Tom Robinson habe Mayella Ewell vergewaltigt, den anschließenden Prozess und Mr Ewells versuchten Mord an Jem.

Schwerpunkte des ersten *Components* sind die Charakterisierung der Hauptfiguren des Romans und Aufgabenstellungen bzw. Informationen zur *Great Depression.*

Zur Sicherung des inhaltlichen Textverständnisses erhalten die Schüler als Hausaufgabe zu jedem Kapitel *while-reading*-Aufgaben *(Copy 1; Copy 2)*. Als *regular homework* sollen die Schüler während der Lektüre des gesamten Romans einen *grid* zum Themenkomplex *Legal terms* anlegen. Dabei können die Begriffe *lawyer, witness, defendant, judge, trial, punishment, lawmaking,* etc. vorkommen, die selbstverständlich beliebig ergänzt werden können.

Lösungen zu Copy 1:

Chapters 1 and 2:
across: 1 distaste; 5 highstrung; 7 detention; 8 ancestor; **down:** 2 to wriggle; 3 telescope; 4 customary; 6 skinny

Chapters 3 and 4
1. involvement, 2. begrudge, 3. auspicious, 4. sluggish, 5. disgrace, 6. villain, 7. erratic, 8. arbitrate

Chapters 5, 6 and 7
to nag: to keep asking someone to do something or to keep complaining to someone about their behaviour in an annoying way
benign: kind and gentle
pulpit: a raised structure at the front of a church that a priest or minister stands on when they speak to the people
to trudge along: to walk with slow, heavy steps
to witness: to see sth happen, especially a crime or an accident
cross examination: the interrogation of a witness called to the stand by one's opponent
to beckon: to make a signal to someone with your hand
desolate: looking empty and sad because there are no people there
moody: annoyed or unhappy
to flunk: to fail a test
grim: making you feel worried or unhappy
vigil: a period of time, especially during the night, when you stay

While-reading chapters 1–11

Complete the given assignments to study the new words.

Chapters 1 and 2

A crossword puzzle

Across
1 Dislike
5 At great tension
7 Maintainance of a person in custody or confinement
8 A person from whom one is descended

Down
2 To twist to and fro
3 An optical instrument for making distant objects appear larger and therefore nearer
4 Usual
6 Very lean or thin

Chapters 3 and 4

Insert the correct words into the given sentences: disgrace – involvement – begrudge – villain – erratic – sluggish – arbitrate – auspicious

1. School officials say they welcome the parental _____.
2. We shouldn't _____ her this success.
3. David Garrett's excellent recording is an _____ start to what promises to be a distinguished musical career.
4. Alex woke late feeling tired and _____.
5. His actions brought _____ on the family.
6. A _____ is a person or thing that has caused all the trouble in a particular situation.
7. His breathing was becoming _____.
8. A committee will _____ between management and the unions.

Chapters 5, 6 and 7

Find the corresponding definitions for the following words.

Chapter 5	1 a period of time, especially during the night, when you stay awake in order to pray, remain with someone who is ill, or watch for danger
to nag	2 to keep asking someone to do something or to keep complaining to someone about their behaviour in an annoying way
benign	3 depressed, unhappy, temperamental
pulpit	4 to see sth happen, especially a crime or an accident
to trudge along	
Chapter 6	5 kind and gentle
to witness	6 to walk with slow, heavy steps
cross examination	7 the interrogation of a witness called to the stand by one's opposing council
to beckon	
desolate	
Chapter 7	8 dismal, gloomy, serious
moody	9 looking empty and sad because there are no people there
to flunk	10 to make a signal to someone with your hand
grim	11 a raised structure at the front of a church that a priest or minister stands on when they speak to the people
vigil	12 to fail a test

Chapter 8 and 9

Find a definition for the following words:
unfathomable – laundry hamper – to scurry – perplexity – dizziness – disgrace – to hoot – obstreperous

Chapters 10 and 11

A crossword puzzle

Across
1 The area of hard skin around the base of your nails
5 To make something unable to operate normally
7 Unable to think clearly, especially because of a shock, accident, etc.
8 Sharp and unkind

Down
2 To shout loudly
3 To keep someone or something within the limits of a particular activity or subject
4 Extremely weak
6 Someone who is unable to stop taking drugs

While-reading tasks: Chapters 1–11

While reading chapters 1 to 11, answer the following questions. Indicate the page(s) and line(s) where you found the answer.

Chapter 1:
1. How many brothers and sisters did Atticus Finch have and what did they do?
2. What do we learn about Dill?
3. What is the description Jem gave of Boo?

Chapter 2:
1. Why was Miss Caroline very annoyed at Scout?
2. What did Scout try to make clear by saying about Walter: "he's a Cunningham"?

Chapter 3:
1. What suggestion did Jem make to Walter and what was Walter's reaction to it?
2. Why was Burris Ewell sent home from school?
3. What was Atticus's opinion about the Ewells?

Chapter 4:
1. What did Scout see in a live oak at the edge of the Radley lot one afternoon after school?
2. Describe the game Jem, Scout and Dill made up during the summer.
3. How did Atticus react when he caught the children playing the Radley family?

Chapter 5:
1. Give a short characterization of Miss Maudie.
2. What did Miss Maudie tell the children about Boo Radley?
3. Describe the children's plan for Boo Radley and Atticus's reaction to it.

Chapter 6:
1. What happened to the children when they went into the Radley lot another time?
2. Why did Jem want to look for his pants at the fence?

Chapter 7:
1. Why was Scout not upset about Jem not speaking for several days?
2. What effect did studying the Egyptians have on Jem?
3. Why were the children so excited about the knothole in the tree and what happened to it in the end?

Chapter 8:
1. Why was snow so fascinating for the children and how did they manage to build a snowman?
2. What happened to Miss Maudie's house that night?
3. Who wrapped a blanket around Scout when she was watching the fire?
4. Describe Miss Maudie's reaction to the burning down of her house.

Chapter 9:
1. In what way did Cecil Jacobs try to provoke Scout?
2. Name the reasons for Atticus deciding to defend Tom Robinson.
3. Mention some peculiarities about the way the house in Finch's Landing was built.
4. What did Francis tell Scout about Atticus and what happened between them afterwards?
5. In what way did Scout and Atticus teach Uncle Jack a lesson?

Chapter 10:
1. Name some of the reasons why Atticus's children thought he was a father who differed considerably from other fathers.
2. In what way did Atticus impress his children?
3. Why did Atticus never tell his children that he was so good at shooting?

Chapter 11:
1. Why did the children hate Mrs Dubose?
2. What was Jem's punishment after he had cut off all the tops of Mrs Dubose's camellia bushes?
3. Why did Mrs Dubose want the children to read to her?

awake in order to pray, remain with someone who is ill, or watch for danger

Chapters 8 and 9:
unfathomable – difficult or impossible to understand
laundry hamper – a household receptacle/container for dirty clothing
to scurry – to move quickly or in haste
perplexity – a tangled or confused situation or condition
dizziness – a sensation of whirling and the feeling of being about to fall
disgrace – the loss of respect, honour, or esteem
to hoot – to assail/scream at with shouts of disapproval or derision
obstreperous – unruly, difficult to control

Chapters 10 and 11:
across: 1 cuticle; 5 to paralyze; 7 dazed; 8 tart; **down:** 2 to holler; 3 to confine; 4 feeble; 6 addict

Lösungen zu Copy 2:

Chapter 1:
1. Atticus went to Montgomery to read law; his younger brother went to Boston to study medicine. Their sister Alexandra remained at the Landing. (p. 5, ll. 1–5)
2. Dill was from Meridian, Mississippi, and was spending the summer with his aunt. His family was from Maycomb originally and his mother worked for a photographer in Meridian. He did not live with his father. (p. 8, ll. 29–33; p. 9, ll. 17–23)
3. Boo was about six-and-a-half feet tall, dined on raw squirrels and any cats he could catch. There was a long jagged scar that ran across his face. His teeth were yellow and rotten. His eyes popped. (p. 16, ll. 11–18)

Chapter 2:
1. Because she discovered that Scout was literate. (p. 22, ll. 17–20)
2. It was clear that Walter was lying about his lunch and that he would never bring any lunch to school. He wouldn't take anything they couldn't pay back. (p. 25, ll. 19–33; p. 26, ll. 1–29)

Chapter 3:
1. He invited him to dinner with them and Walter only accepted very late after some convincing. (p. 30, ll. 22f.; p. 31, ll. 1–11)
2. Because Miss Caroline was shocked to see that he had bugs in his hair. (p. 34, ll. 11–18)
3. He said that they had been the disgrace of Maycomb for three generations. None of them had done any honest work. They were people, but they lived like animals. (p. 40, ll. 19–30)

Chapter 4:
1. She saw two pieces of chewing gum in a hole. (p. 44, ll. 16–20)
2. Scout was to act as Mrs Radley. Dill was old Mr Radley. Jem was Boo: he went under the front steps and shrieked and howled from time to time. (p. 51, ll. 32f.; p. 52, ll. 1–4)
3. He disapproved of it and took the scissors away from them. (p. 53, ll. 30–33; p. 54, ll. 1f.)

Chapter 5:
1. She let the children play on her lawn, hated her house and spent as

little time as possible indoors. She was on a permanent crusade against nut grass. (p. 56, ll. 4–22)

2. She said that there was a lot of gossip about him, three-fourths colored folks and one-fourth Stephanie Crawford. Boo Radley spoke nicely to her when he was a boy and she also said that he was probably crazy by now. (p. 60, ll. 22–33; p. 61, ll. 1–9)

3. They wanted to put a note on the end of a fishing pole and stick it to the shutters of the Radley house. When Dill was ringing the bell to indicate danger, Atticus told them to leave Boo Radley alone. (p. 63, ll. 20–33; p. 64, ll. 1–28; p. 65, ll. 6ff.)

Chapter 6:

1. They saw a shadow, heard the roar of a shotgun and escaped through the fence. (p. 71, ll. 13–33; p. 72, ll. 1–5)

2. He had lied to Atticus about the reason why he had lost them and he did not want him to become suspicious. (p. 74, ll. 29–32; p. 75, ll. 1–23)

Chapter 7:

1. She tried to climb into Jem's skin and understand his Radley adventure. (p. 77, ll. 1–6)

2. He tried to walk flat a great deal, sticking one arm in front of him and one in back of him putting one foot behind the other. He was very impressed by their accomplishments. (p. 79, ll. 13–21)

3. They found little things for them in it (small images carved in soap, a packet of chewing gum, a tarnished medal, etc.) but after some time the knot-hole had been filled with cement. (p. 80, ll. 8–15; p. 80, ll. 32f.; p. 81, ll. 1–4; p. 81, ll. 11–14; p. 83, ll. 3–8)

Chapter 8:

1. They had never seen snow before. Then they gathered all the snow they could find from the back yard to the front. Jem constructed a torso of dirt and plastered it with snow. He used bits of wood for eyes, nose, mouth, buttons and a stick of stovewood. (p. 86, ll. 6–11; p. 88, ll. 17–34; p. 89, ll. 1–30)

2. It burned down completely. (p. 92, ll. 7–end; p. 93; p. 94; p. 95, ll. 1ff.)

3. Boo Radley (p. 96, ll. 17f.)

4. She was not grieving and even seemed to be relieved. She said that she had thought of setting fire to it herself. She wanted to build a smaller house with a big yard to have more room for her azaleas. (p. 97, ll. 5–13)

Chapter 9:

1. He said that her father defended niggers. (p. 99, ll. 9ff.)

2. Atticus explained that if he did not defend Tom he would not be able to hold his head up, or to represent his country in the legislature, or to tell Scout or Jem to do anything again. He felt personally affected by the case and believed he had the moral duty to act. (p. 100, ll. 25–33; p. 101, ll. 1–9)

3. The daughters' rooms could be reached only by one staircase, Welcome's room and the guestroom only by another, the kitchen was separated from the rest of the house, tacked onto it by a wooden catwalk and there was a widow's walk on the roof. (p. 106, ll. 23–33; p. 107, l. 1f.)

4. He said Atticus let Jem and Scout run around with stray dogs and that

Atticus was a niggerlover. This led Scout and him to start fighting and in the end, Scout and Jem had to drive home. (p. 110, ll. 8–33; p. 111; p. 112, ll. 1–29)

5. Scout told him that he didn't understand children much because, before interfering, he should have also listened to her side of it. Atticus told him that he should not answer in an evasive way when asked something. (p. 113, ll. 17–33; p. 114, ll. 1 f.; p. 116, ll. 1–8)

Chapter 10:

1. He did not do anything that could possibly arouse the admiration of anyone. He never went hunting, did not play poker or fish or drink or smoke, he just read. Atticus did not take part in the game of touch football. (p. 118, ll. 11–22; p. 121, ll. 27–33; p. 122, ll. 1–4)

2. He killed the old mad dog Tim Johnson with one shot. (p. 127, ll. 9–33; p. 128, ll. 1–22)

3. Atticus thought that God had given him an unfair advantage over most living things. He wasn't particularly proud of his abilities. (p. 130, ll. 11–18)

Chapter 11:

1. Because she raked them with her wrathful gaze, subjected them to ruthless interrogation regarding their behaviour and they could do nothing to please her. (p. 132, ll. 19–23; p. 133, ll. 1–4)

2. He had to come every afternoon after school and Saturdays and read to her out loud for two hours. He had to do it for a month. (p. 140, ll. 20–25)

3. Because she was a morphine addict and while the children were reading she did not allow herself any morphine to break the addiction. (p. 147, ll. 27–33; p. 148, ll. 1–9)

Bevor der Themenkomplex *characterization* erarbeitet wird, sollten die ersten elf Kapitel des Buches von den Schülerinnen und Schülern gelesen worden sein.

 Als Einstieg in die erste Stunde wird die Einstiegsseite in den Mittelpunkt gerückt, die das Thema *outsider* grafisch darstellt. Dazu wird in einem *brainstorming* eine *mind map* zu diesem Thema erarbeitet. Daher könnte angesichts der Tatsache, dass die Schüler die ersten elf Kapitel bereits gelesen haben, folgender Erwartungshorizont denkbar sein:

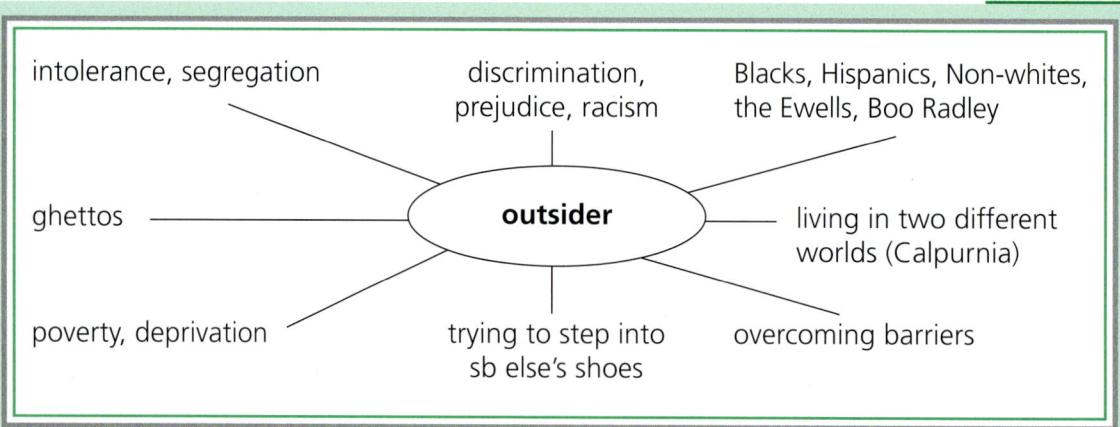

In einem sich anschließenden Unterrichtsgespräch kann auf die im Roman dargestellte Situation eingegangen werden. Insofern werden einige der herausragenden Vertreter der verschiedenen Gruppierungen kurz beleuchtet und auf eine eventuelle Außenseiterrolle hin untersucht. In diesem Zusammenhang können die Ewells, die Radley-Familie, Calpurnia und

Tom Robinson mit seiner Familie erwähnt werden, während Atticus mit seiner Familie, Miss Maudie, Miss Crawford, Mrs Dubose usw. von ihrem Hintergrund her als allgemein akzeptierte Mitglieder der Gesellschaft angesehen werden. Dagegen stehen die Ewells als die weißen *underdogs,* die Radley-Familie und besonders Boo als mysteriös und unnahbar, Calpurnia als Vertreterin der *Negroes,* die Zugang zur weißen Gesellschaft erhält, und Tom Robinson als Schwarzer, der nicht nur wegen seiner Hautfarbe ausgegrenzt ist, sondern zusätzlich noch eines Verbrechens bezichtigt wird.

Nachdem eine Textverständnissicherung der ersten drei Kapitel durch die zugehörigen Aufgabenstellungen zur Wortschatzarbeit und die entsprechenden *while-reading*-Fragen erfolgt ist *(Copy 1* und *Copy 2),* richtet sich der Schwerpunkt nun auf eine systematische Annäherung an den Themenkomplex *character and characterization.* Die Schüler sollen sich zunächst einen allgemeinen Überblick über die Möglichkeiten eines Autors verschaffen, eine Figur zu charakterisieren *(showing and telling technique).* Ausgehend von den auf Folie oder Tafel präsentierten einfachen, eindeutigen Beispielen gelangen die Schüler in einem Unterrichtsgespräch zu der Erkenntnis, dass ein fiktionaler Charakter direkt oder indirekt vom Autor gezeichnet werden kann. Als Ergebnis kann sich das folgende Folien- bzw. Tafelbild ergeben.

Describe the differences between these two ways of characterizing a person.

Walter Cunningham's face told everybody in the first grade he had hookworms. His absence of shoes told us how he got them. People caught hookworms going barefoot in barnyards and hog wallows. If Walter had owned any shoes, he would have worn them the first day of school and then discarded them until mid-winter. He did have on a clean shirt and neatly mended overalls.

➡ **direct characterization "telling techniques"**

The author informs the reader about the characteristic traits of a person

Jem suddenly grinned at him. "Come on home to dinner with us, Walter," he said. "We'd be glad to have you." Walter's face brightened, then darkened. … Walter stood where he was, biting his lip. (p. 30, l. 22 – p. 31, l. 9)

➡ **indirect characterization "showing techniques"**

The reader has to infer what a character is like by interpreting his behaviour or his words.

Zur Vertiefung und zur Verdeutlichung, dass ein Autor innerhalb eines Werkes mit beiden Techniken arbeiten kann, wie im obigen Beispiel schon gezeigt, werden die Schülerinnen und Schüler nun aufgefordert, ein Beispiel für jede der Techniken in *Chapter 1* zu finden.

Find an example in chapter 1 where Lee uses the telling technique and an example where she uses the showing technique to let the reader know what a character is like.

Zum Beispiel könnten folgende Stellen des Romans genannt werden:

Telling technique:
- "Jem wanted Dill to know once and for all that he wasn't scared of anything: 'It's just that I can't think of a way to make him come out

without him getting us.' Besides, Jem had his little sister to think of."
(p. 17, ll. 15–18)

- "The Radley Place fascinated Dill. In spite of our warnings and explanations it drew him as the moon draws water, but drew him no nearer than the light-pole on the corner, a safe distance from the Radley gate." (p. 10, ll. 7–10)

Showing technique:

- "'I'm Charles Baker Harris,' he said. 'I can read. 'So what?' I said. 'I just thought you'd like to know I can read. You got anything needs readin' I can do it. …'" (p. 8, ll. 7–10)
- "'There goes the meanest man ever God blew breath into,' murmured Calpurnia, and she spat meditatively into the yard." (p. 15, ll. 15 ff.)

Im Anschluss daran können in einem Unterrichtsgespräch die Aspekte herausgestellt werden, die für eine Charakterisierung wesentlich sind. Die Ergebnisse werden in Form eines *clusters* an der Tafel festgehalten, brauchen aber nicht von den Schülern abgeschrieben zu werden, da sie auf der Kopiervorlage *Characterization (Copy 3)* abgedruckt sind.

Hilfreich ist es in diesem Zusammenhang auch, den Schülerinnen und Schülern Vokabellisten zum Thema *characterization* an die Hand zu geben. Diese sind auf *Copy 5* zu finden.

 Which aspects can give us information about a person's character?

 Als Hausaufgabe für die nächste Stunde sollen die auf Kapitel 4 bis 6 bezogenen Aufgabenstellungen zur Wortschatzarbeit und die entsprechenden *while-reading questions* bearbeitet werden *(Copy 1; Copy 2)*.

 Nachdem die für eine Charakterisierung wesentlichen Aspekte herausgestellt worden sind, soll nun eine Charakterisierung von Scout auf der Basis der ersten elf Kapitel angelegt werden. Diese soll in der Art eines *character file* erfolgen, der als Kopiervorlage *(Copy 4)* vorgegeben wird. Die Erarbeitung erfolgt in Partnerarbeit. Alle wichtigen Informationen, die die Schülerinnen und Schüler explizit oder implizit zu Scout finden, sollen in die passende Rubrik eingetragen werden, damit man sich ein genaues Bild von der Protagonistin machen kann. Es ist wichtig, darauf hinzuweisen, dass diese Einträge nur ein Anfang sind und dass die Aufzeichnungen beim weiteren Lesen kontinuierlich ergänzt werden sollen (gegebenenfalls auf zusätzlichen Blättern). Den Schülerinnen und Schülern soll erläutert werden, dass die Aufzeichnungen später verwendet werden, wenn es im weiteren Verlauf des Romans darum geht, Scouts Entwicklung zu besprechen.

Im Anschluss an die Partnerarbeit finden sich die Schülerinnen und Schüler in Kleingruppen zusammen, vergleichen ihre Ausarbeitungen und bestimmen ein Gruppenmitglied, das die Ergebnisse dem Kurs präsentiert.

  Work together in groups, then compare your results and present them to the class.

Die gleiche Aufgabenstellung auf der Basis des *character file* kann selbstverständlich auch für Atticus, Jem oder eine andere zentrale Figur im Roman durchgeführt werden. Es ist jedoch nicht ratsam, diese Aufgabenstellung zu sehr auszudehnen, also auf mehr als zwei Personen anzuwenden.

 Als Hausaufgabe sollen die Schülerinnen und Schüler die auf Kapitel 7 bis 9 bezogenen Aufgabenstellungen zur Wortschatzarbeit und die zugehörigen *while-reading questions* bearbeiten *(Copy 1; Copy 2)*.

Character and characterization

Characters are the persons, in a dramatic or narrative work, endowed with moral and dispositional qualities that are expressed in what they say and what they do. The grounds in a character's temperament and moral nature for his speech and actions determine his motivation. A character may be timid, self-assured, ambitious, polite, ruthless, and so on. In **drama**, the qualities of characters might be shown by means of their appearance, actions, language, thoughts, interaction or hearsay. In **fiction**, an author has more refined ways of presenting a character, since he/she can make use of a narrator. A character may remain essentially "stable", or unchanged in his/her outlook and dispositions, from the beginning to the end of a work (Atticus in *To Kill a Mockingbird*), or he may undergo a radical change, either through a gradual development or as the result of an extreme crisis (Austin in *True West*).

Round characters and flat characters
A round character (also called "dynamic") is complex in temperament and motivation and is represented with subtle particularities; thus he/she is as difficult to describe with any adequacy as a person in real life, and, like most people, he/she is capable of surprising us. He/she develops in the course of the story.
A flat character (also called a "type", "two-dimensional", or "static"), is built around a single idea or quality and is presented in outline and without much individualising detail and can thus be fairly adequately described in a single phrase or sentence. He/she does not change or develop in the story.

Showing technique and telling technique
Showing techniques (also called "indirect characterization") are almost the same as those used by a dramatist (appearance, actions, language, thoughts, interaction). The author merely presents his/her characters talking and acting in different situations and leaves the reader to infer what motives and dispositions lie behind what they say and do. With telling techniques (also called "direct characterization"), the author informs the reader more directly about what characters are like, analyzing and summarizing their characteristic traits, usually by means of the narrator.

Aspects of characterization

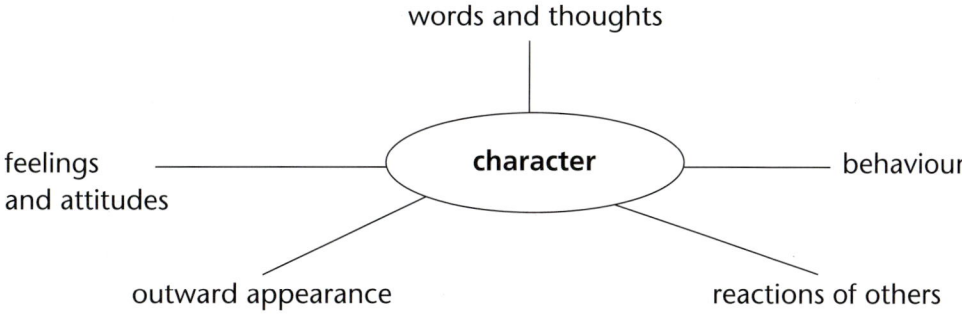

Character file: Scout

Write down all the important information you get from the first 11 chapters about Scout. Remember that an author can present a character in a **direct** or an **indirect** way.
Make sure you work on this file continuously as you will find new information each time you read another chapter. You will also see that the character develops in the course of the novel.

General information (age, profession, family background, interests, etc.)

Appearance (eyes, hair, face, clothes, etc.)

Character traits (good and bad character traits, talents, etc.)

Behaviour (relationships with other people, actions/reactions, etc.)

Way of thinking (opinions, etc.)

Other information

Useful phrases and words for characterizations

The author	describes	the characteristics	of
		outward appearance	
		intellectual qualities	
		mood	
		activities	
		social and psychological condition	

points out the characteristics of …
gives a characterization of …
characterizes … (a person as …)
          realistic
gives a detailed description of
only gives a rough description of …

the character is	described	as
	presented	
	characterized	

the basic traits of A's character are …
one of A's striking characteristics is …
A stands in clear contrast to B

Behaviour

to show	good	behaviour towards …
	bad	
	polite	
	impolite	

to behave	well
	badly
	politely

to control/discipline one's behaviour

sb's behaviour is	upstanding
	eccentric
	naughty
	nasty
	infamous
	impudent

to reprove	sb for his/her behaviour
blame	
criticize	

to feel sympathy towards sb

Character traits

self-controlled	easily excited
balanced	irritable
calm	impulsive
patient	intemperate
moderate	impatient
tolerant	bad-tempered
friendly	intolerant
good-natured	benevolent
sensitive	cruel
modest	brutal
self-centered	obstinate
aggressive	stubborn

Feelings

to feel	pricks of conscience
	guilty
	innocent
	repentant

to be sorry for …

to have a	guilty	conscience
	troubled	
	tortured	

to be/feel	hopeful	optimistic
	confident	courageous
	desperate	pessimistic
	fearful	

Lösungsvorschlag zu Copy 4 (unter Zugrundelegung der Kapitel 1 bis 5):

General Information (age, profession, family background, interests, etc.)
- almost six (ch. 1, p. 7)
- Scout's mother died of a heart attack when Scout was two; she has no memories of her (ch. 1, p. 7)
- Atticus Finch, her father, is a lawyer
- eager to investigate the Radley Place (ch. 4, pp. 44 – 50)

Appearance (eyes, hair, face, clothes, etc.)
- tomboy, plays the same games as the boys and does not act in a ladylike way or like a little girl (ch. 4, pp. 44 ff.)

Character traits (good and bad character traits, talents, etc.)
- intelligent and precocious child who learned how to read through her natural instincts (ch. 2, pp. 22 f.)
- acts as a spokesperson for her entire class, interacting with the adult teacher comfortably (more grown-up than some of her peers) (ch. 2, p. 26)

Behaviour (relationships with other people, actions/reactions, etc.)
- tries to explain to Miss Caroline the peculiarities of the Cunningham family, thus displaying a certain degree of maturity (ch. 2, p. 26)
- is rude towards Walter Cunningham during dinner (ch. 3, p. 32)
- wants to find answers to her questions about Boo by taking part in the drama game (ch. 4, pp. 51 ff.) and by participating in passing a note to Boo at the Radley place telling him that they want to befriend him (ch. 5, pp. 63 ff.)
- though still frightened of Boo, she wishes to befriend him and help him (ch. 5, pp. 61 ff.)

Way of thinking (opinions, etc.)
- is fascinated by the Radley house and the mysterious Boo and is prepared to take part in efforts to approach it (ch. 1, pp. 14 ff.)
- finds her father 'satisfactory' and Calpurnia 'tyrannical' (ch. 1, pp. 6 f.)
- often looks up to Atticus, who always displays an upright, morally-sound response for his reactions to events (ch. 1, pp. 13 ff.; ch. 3, pp. 39 – 42)
- feels frustrated at being reprimanded by her teacher for having been taught to read and write (ch. 2, pp. 22 ff.)
- finds school boring (ch. 4, pp. 43 f.)
- is terrified by Boo's mystery (ch. 4, pp. 50 f.)
- respects and is friendly with Miss Maudie as a motherly influence (ch. 5, pp. 56 – 60)

Other information
- Boo Radley puts little objects in the knothole of a tree as a gift for Scout and Jem as he likes them (ch. 4, p. 44)
- Jem classifies her as "girlish" (ch. 6, p. 69)
- Aunt Alexandra tells Scout that she should be more ladylike, should wear dresses and not pants, and that she should play with girls' toys like tea sets and jewelry (ch. 9, p. 108)

In der anschließenden Unterrichtsstunde wird eine ausführliche Charakterisierung von Scout auf der Basis der bisher zusammengetragenen Information des *character file* und weiterer Informationen aus den folgenden Kapiteln des ersten Teils des Buches in Form eines zusammenhängenden Textes ausgearbeitet. Ein ausführlicher Lösungsvorschlag wird den Schülerinnen und Schülern in *Copy 6* an die Hand gegeben.

Model characterization of Scout

Scout is Atticus Finch's daughter. Atticus is a lawyer and they live in a small town in Southern Alabama. Scout is almost six and her brother Jem almost ten. Her mother died of a heart attack when she was two, so she has hardly any memories of her. She behaves like a tomboy, always playing the same games as her brother
5 and their mutual friend Dill and not acting like a ladylike little girl.
On the contrary, she always insists on taking part in the adventurous games of the other two, for example, trying to find out about the Radley Place. The Radley family is a somewhat mysterious family who live in a rather secluded way and are therefore of prominent interest to the children. Scout wants to find answers to her
10 questions about Boo Radley by taking part in the drama game and by participating in passing a note to Boo at the Radley Place telling him that she and the boys want to befriend and help him. She is thus fascinated by the Radley Place and the mysterious Boo and is therefore prepared to take part in efforts to approach it, e.g. by rolling towards it in a tyre.
15 Scout often looks up to Atticus, who always displays an upright, morally-sound response for his reactions to events and who can always be relied on to provide sensible explanations to his children's questions. She finds her father 'satisfactory', but Calpurnia 'tyrannical'. On the other hand, she thinks her father cannot do anything besides being a lawyer as he does not do hands-on physical work and he
20 does not play football. He is also much older than the parents of her peers, but when Atticus shoots the mad stray-dog with one shot, she is very proud of him. Moreover, she defends her father when other children drop nasty comments about his decision to defend the accused Tom Robinson.
She is an intelligent and precocious child who learned how to read through her
25 natural instincts and feels frustrated at being reprimanded by her teacher for having already been taught. At the beginning of the school year, she tries to explain to Miss Caroline the peculiarities of the Cunningham family, thus displaying a certain degree of maturity and acts as a spokesperson for her entire class, interacting comfortably with the adult teacher. Altogether, school is boring for her. The
30 school may be attempting to turn the children into moral beings, but Scout's moral education occurs almost exclusively in her home or in the presence of Maycomb adults and friends. In this respect she looks up to and is friendly with Miss Maudie as a motherly influence whereas she does not like her Aunt Alexandra because she always tells her that she should behave in a more ladylike way.
35 In conclusion, one can say that at the beginning of the novel, Scout lives a relatively sheltered and innocent life and is a child who is curious and inquisitive about her environment. In the course of the novel, she is gradually confronted with the more serious problems of that particular time of the Great Depression in the 30s, such as racism and hypocrisy.

> Write a characterization of Scout based on the findings of the *character file* and the information from the first part of the novel.

Die Hausaufgabe zur nächsten Stunde besteht darin, die **Charakterisierung** zu Ende zu schreiben und die auf Kapitel 10 und 11 bezogenen Aufgaben zur Wortschatzarbeit und die *while-reading assignments* zu bearbeiten (Copy 1; Copy 2).

1.2 The Great Depression – ramifications in Maycomb and America in general

Zunächst wird die Hausaufgabe vorgetragen, um die inhaltliche Sicherung des ersten Teils des Romans abzuschließen.

Im Weiteren liegt der Schwerpunkt der unterrichtlichen Erarbeitung auf der Ära der *Great Depression* in den USA in den Dreißigerjahren des 20. Jahrhunderts, in deren Folge der sogenannte *New Deal* von Präsident F. D. Roosevelt eingeführt wurde. Diese Epoche gewinnt eine neue aktuelle Dimension durch die gegenwärtige (Winter 2008/09) und virulente Bankenkrise in den USA, die durch unkontrollierte Spekulationen und ungezügeltes *investment banking* hervorgerufen wurde und die sich nun auf viele andere Länder auswirkt. Die konkreten Folgen für die betroffenen Länder sind bisher noch nicht absehbar.

An den Anfang dieser Erarbeitung werden zwei Textstellen aus dem ersten Teil des Romans gestellt, die laut vorgelesen und anschließend auf Informationen hin untersucht werden, die deutlich im Zusammenhang mit den schwierigen wirtschaftlichen Verhältnissen stehen. Im Anschluss daran wird ein größerer Bogen zur *Great Depression* geschlagen, in dessen Abfolge Material wie zum Beispiel Fotos, Zeitungsartikel über die damalige und auch heutige Bankensituation und allgemeine Informationen *(fact files)* über diese Zeit gesammelt und analysiert werden.

> Read the passages in the book from p. 25, l. 6 to p. 28, l. 9 and p. 30, l. 17 to p. 32, l. 23 aloud and collect all the descriptions pointing to an economically difficult time for the Cunningham family and others. Work in groups.

Descriptions indicating an economically difficult era

- Walter does not have money for school lunch
- Walter does not have shoes to wear and therefore has hookworms
- Walter cannot pass first grade because he has to help around the farm
- Walter and Atticus talk about farm problems
- Walter displays somewhat rough table manners, which Scout comments on critically
- Mr Cunningham is struggling with payments for mortgages on his land
- the children anxiously want to know if they are "poor"
- doctors, dentists and lawyers get little payment for their services
- Mr Cunningham does not have any money to pay Atticus back for his services
  However
- The Cunninghams never take anything they cannot pay back so Mr Cunningham supplies Atticus with farm goods

⇒ the Cunninghams must keep the farm running in order to survive, but the school system does not make any accommodation for farm children, so they stay illiterate

Diese Aufgabe wird in Gruppenarbeit erledigt. Nach dem Vorlesen der Romanauszüge suchen die einzelnen Gruppen die entsprechenden Textstellen heraus und stellen anschließend die Ergebnisse ihrer Arbeit vor.

In einem Unterrichtsgespräch wird nun über weiter reichende Auswirkungen der *Great Depression* in den USA gesprochen. Dazu kann man beispielsweise eines der Fotos als Grundlage nehmen und die auf ihnen abgebildeten Kennzeichen von Armut bzw. armseligen und schwierigen Lebensumständen herausarbeiten. Dies wird an einem Beispiel auf der Kopiervorlage *Working with pictures (Copy 7)* dargestellt. Man kann so vorgehen, dass zunächst die Kopiervorlage besprochen und dann in einem Unterrichtsgespräch die einzelnen Schritte der Interpretation auf das Bild angewendet werden. Als Hausaufgabe wird dann eine schriftliche Ausarbeitung der Bildinterpretation gestellt.

Unemployed men vying[1] for jobs at the American Legion Employment Bureau in Los Angeles during the Great Depression

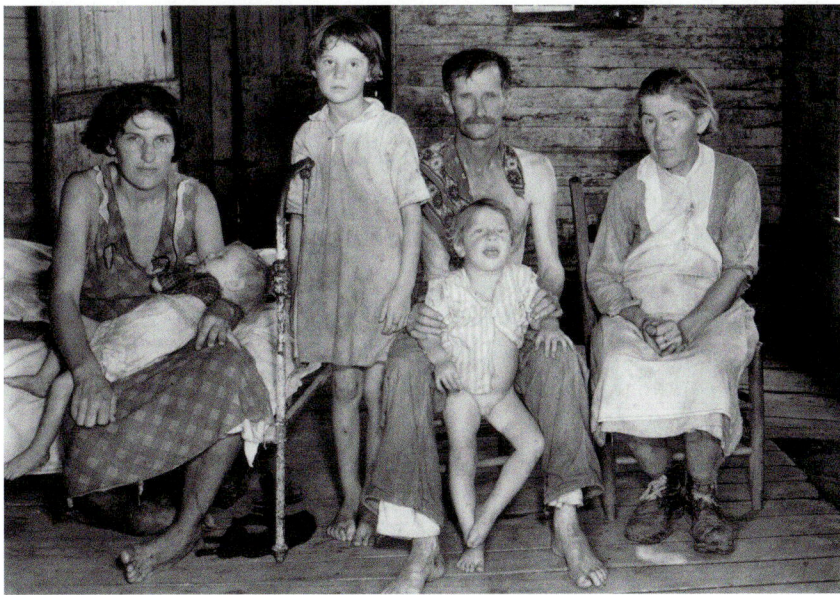

Bud Fields and his family, Alabama. 1935 or 1936

---

[1] **to vie** *wetteifern*

Working with pictures

Pictures can be used to illustrate a certain situation or political opinion or attitude. Their function can be to epitomize a certain statement or criticism of existing grievances or to make a clear point. The following steps can help you to structure the interpretation of a picture.

1. Source and content

Express in a few sentences
- where the picture comes from (e. g. a newspaper, magazine, a personal picture or the Internet)
- what the picture is about or deals with (its theme or subject)

2. Description

Describe all the elements in the picture and point out the relationship between them by
- starting in the foreground and ending with the background
- carefully describing the features of each of the objects or the outward appearance of the figures (e. g. facial expression, gestures, postures, clothing) and their actions

3. Message

Explain what the photographer or the person using the picture wants to say or show by
- examining the caption and the picture together

Vocabulary: Working with Pictures

The picture by ... published in ...	shows/presents depicts deals with /is about	a possible view of/on ... an attitude towards the problem of ...
At first sight the picture is glance	funny/interesting/boring/annoying/confusing/ poignant/full of pathos	

The first impression of the picture is .../What is striking about the picture is ...

The picture consists of several pictorial elements.
The pictorial elements of the picture can easily be distinguished. The first one ...
In the foreground/background   ... is shown/depicted/can be seen

The picture expresses joy/hate/melancholy/sadness/vitality (or other emotions)

The caption	reads/states/plainly shows that ... is unexpected/forms a contrast to the picture

The picture clearly shows ...
It is plain to see/obvious ...
The message of the picture/The photographer's message is ...
What we learn from the picture is ...
The photographer criticizes the situation of/man's irresponsible way of ...

Read the two handouts about "Working with pictures" and clarify their contents.

Nun widmen die Schülerinnen und Schüler ihre Aufmerksamkeit dem Bild *Unemployed men vying for jobs at the American Legion Employment Bureau in Los Angeles during the Great Depression*. Nach einer kurzen Unterrichtsphase, während der sie sich das Bild, welches entweder als Kopie verteilt oder auf dem OHP präsentiert wird, genau anschauen sollen, beginnt die inhaltliche Erarbeitung im Unterrichtsgespräch. Im Folgenden wird ein Erwartungshorizont formuliert, der sich an der auf der Kopiervorlage skizzierten Vorgehensweise orientiert.

Describe and interpret the picture.

Erwartungshorizont:
This picture can be found at the following website address: http://www. english.uiuc.edu/maps/depression/photoessay.htm.
It deals with the situation of the high rate of unemployment in the aftermath of the *Great Depression* in the USA.
At first sight, the picture displays a lively and agitated atmosphere with a lot of commotion. The picture was taken in a room full of men, densely packed together, who are apparently shouting and raising their arms. It consists of several pictorial elements. In the foreground, we can see three men behind a counter who are writing something down. In the middle and in the background, we can see a crowd of men who are all neatly dressed. Some of them are wearing suits with a cap or hat on their heads. They make a clean and well-kept impression. The men are pushing forward and displaying a lot of commotion and agitation. Most of them are raising their hands and trying to get the attention of the three men behind the counter, and some of them are obviously shouting. On the board in the background, we can read the phrase: "Join the American Legion". The American Legion was chartered by the U.S. Congress as a patriotic, mutual-help, wartime veterans organization for members of the United States armed forces who had served during a wartime period. In addition to organizing commemorative events and volunteer activities, the American Legion is still active in US politics, with its primary political activity being lobbying on behalf of the interests of veterans.
If we consider the caption underneath the picture, it becomes clear that these men are all desperately trying to get one of the few jobs available at that time. Some of them might even have worked in more highly-qualified jobs before the Depression but now have to compete for menial jobs.
The invitation written on the board to join the American Legion points to the fact that, at the time in question, there were many veterans that were unemployed or in difficult financial circumstances and who could thereby profit from being a member of this organization.
What we learn from the picture is that the overall atmosphere is not pleasant or happy, but instead if we look closely at some of the men's faces we can detect a certain degree of tension.

Nachdem in der folgenden Stunde die Hausaufgaben vorgetragen wurden, rückt die Ära der *Great Depression* in den USA in den Vordergrund. In diesem Zusammenhang könnte zunächst die Kopiervorlage *(Copy 8)* gemeinsam gelesen werden, die einen inhaltlichen Überblick über die damaligen Ereignisse und ihre Konsequenzen gibt. Die sich anschließenden Texterschließungsfragen dienen der vertiefenden inhaltlichen Erarbeitung. Es ist ratsam, die Kopiervorlage laut vorlesen zu lassen, da sich im Verlaufe des Lesens sicherlich sowohl Verständnis- als auch Vokabelfragen ergeben werden. Insofern kann schon eine Diskussion über die genannten Aspekte eingeleitet werden. Die zugehörigen Textfragen werden anschließend in Gruppenarbeit in schriftlicher Form beantwortet. Jeweils eines der Gruppenmitglieder stellt dann die Ergebnisse vor. Zur zusätzlichen Auseinandersetzung mit dieser Epoche und, wie sich aufgrund der jüngsten Entwicklungen in der US-Finanzwelt herausgestellt hat, mit den aktuellen Konsequenzen der dramatischen Vorgänge in der Wall Street in New York werden die Schülerinnen und Schüler aufgefordert, darüber in Form von Referaten zu berichten. Im Weiteren finden sich einige nützliche Internetadressen zu diesen Aspekten.

Read *Copy 8* about the Great Depression aloud and then answer the given questions. Work in groups. Select one group member to present your findings.

Internetadressen zu *The Great Depression* and *The Wall Street Near-Crash in 2008:*
http://newdeal.feri.org/
http://newdeal.feri.org/texts/publish.htm
http://www.j-bradford-delong.net/tceh/Slouch_Crash14.html
http://www.nytimes.com/2008/09/28/business/28lloyd.html?_r=1&8dpc=&pagewanted=print&oref=slogin
http://lcweb2.loc.gov/learn/features/timeline/depwwii/newdeal/newdeal.html
http://www.guardian.co.uk/business/2008/sep/15/lehmanbrothers.wallstreet
http://www.guardian.co.uk/business/2008/sep/15/marketturmoil.stockmarkets

Lösungsvorschläge zu *Copy 8*:

1. The Great Depression began with a collapse of stock-market prices on the New York Stock Exchange in October 1929. With the stock prices continuing to fall during the next three years they had reached only about 20 percent of their value by late 1932. This development ruined thousands of investors and the decline in the value of assets strained banks and other financial institutions. Therefore many banks were driven into insolvency. The failure of the banks together with an overall loss of confidence in the economy resulted in much-reduced levels of spending and demand and thereby of production. As a consequence, the output was dramatically decreasing and unemployment was rising. By 1932, unemployment had risen to 25–30 per cent of the work force.

2. It turned into a worldwide economic slump because there were close relationships between the United States and European economies after World War I. After the war the United States had acted as the major creditor and financier of postwar Europe, whose national economies had been greatly affected by the war itself and war debts.

3. The economic distress resulted in the election of the Democrat Franklin D. Rooselvelt as President in late 1932. He introduced many changes in the structure of the American economy making use of

more government regulation and a variety of public-works projects to assist to a recovery. As market forces alone had proved unable to achieve the desired recovery during the Great Depression, government action came to play an important role in ensuring economic stability in many industrial nations with market economies.

4. 1. The nation's banks were first closed and only reopened if they were solvent.
   2. A policy of moderate currency inflation was adopted to start an upward movement in commodity prices and to afford relief to debtors.
   3. Generous credit facilities were offered to industry and agriculture.
   4. Savings-bank deposits were insured up to $ 5,000 and severe regulations were forced upon the sale of securities on the stock exchange.
   5. The Civilian Conservation Corps (CCC) was introduced which enrolled jobless young men in work camps across the country.
   6. The Civil Works Administration provided work relief in terms of funding jobs.

5. The Agricultural Adjustment Act (AAA) provided economic relief to farmers. The plan was to raise crop prices by paying farmers a subsidy to compensate for voluntary cutbacks in production. The payments would be funded by a tax imposed on industries that processed crops. Consequently, the output dropped which was also a result of the Commodity Credit Corporation, a program which extended loans for crops kept off the market.

6. 1. The Works Progress Administration (WPA) which was created under the second New Deal was geared at providing work rather than welfare. Accordingly, buildings, roads, airports and schools were constructed.
   2. Via the Federal Theater Project, the Federal Art Project and the Federal Writers Project actors, painters, musicians and writers were employed.
   3. The National Youth Administration provided part-time employment to students, implemented training programs and offered aid to umemployed young people.
   Generally, Americans wanted the government to take greater responsibility for the welfare of the nation. Therefore the New Deal has been credited with laying the foundations of the modern welfare state in the United States.

7. President Roosevelt was of the opinion that measures fostering economic well-being would strengthen liberty and democracy. He thought that in other nations the disappearance of democracy had been due to the citizens' tiredness of unemployment, insecurity and hunger in the face of government weakness. Therefore he wanted to preserve the democratic institutions by protecting the security of the people, especially the economic security. This implied the introduction of various measures providing the people with the means of keeping up a decent lifestyle.

The Great Depression – fact file

The Great Depression was an economic slump in North America, Europe, and other industrialized areas of the world that began in 1929 and lasted until about 1939. It was the longest and most severe depression ever experienced by the industrialized Western world.

Though the U.S. economy had gone into depression six months earlier, the Great Depression may be said to have begun with a catastrophic collapse of stock-market prices on the New York Stock Exchange in October 1929. During the next three years, stock prices in the United States continued to fall, until by late 1932, they had dropped to only about 20 percent of their value in 1929. Besides ruining many thousands of individual investors, this precipitous decline in the value of assets greatly strained banks and other financial institutions, particularly those holding stocks in their portfolios. Many banks were consequently forced into insolvency; by 1933, 11,000 of the United States' 25,000 banks had failed. The failure of so many banks, combined with a general and nationwide loss of confidence in the economy, led to much-reduced levels of spending and demand and hence of production, thus aggravating the downward spiral. The result was drastically falling output and drastically rising unemployment; by 1932, U.S. manufacturing output had fallen to 54 percent of its 1929 level, and unemployment had risen to between 12 and 15 million workers, or 25–30 percent of the work force.

The Great Depression began in the United States but quickly turned into a worldwide economic slump, owing to the special and intimate relationships that had been forged between the United States and European economies after World War I. The United States had emerged from the war as the major creditor and financier of postwar Europe, whose national economies had been greatly weakened by the war itself, by war debts, and, in the case of Germany and other defeated nations, by the need to pay war reparations.

The Great Depression had important consequences in the political sphere. In the United States, economic distress led to the election of the Democrat Franklin D. Roosevelt to the presidency in late 1932. Roosevelt introduced a number of major changes in the structure of the American economy, using increased government regulation and massive public-works projects to promote a recovery. But despite this active intervention, mass unemployment and economic stagnation continued, though on a somewhat reduced scale, with about 15 percent of the work force still unemployed in 1939 at the outbreak of World War II.

At least in part, the Great Depression was caused by underlying weaknesses and imbalances within the U.S. economy that had been obscured by the boom psychology and speculative euphoria of the 1920s. The Depression exposed those weaknesses, as it did the inability of the nation's political and financial institutions to cope with the vicious downward economic cycle that had set in by 1930. Prior to the Great Depression, governments traditionally took little or no action in times of business downturn, relying instead on impersonal market forces to achieve the necessary economic correction. But market forces alone proved unable to achieve the desired recovery in the early years of the Great Depression, and this painful discovery eventually inspired some fundamental changes in the United States' economic structure. After the Great Depression, government action, whether in the form of taxation, industrial regulation, public works, social insurance, social-welfare services, or deficit spending, came to assume a principal role in ensuring economic stability in most industrial nations with market economies.

Roosevelt and the New Deal

In 1933, the new president, Franklin Roosevelt, brought an air of confidence and optimism that quickly rallied the people to the banner of his program, known as the New Deal. "The only thing we have to fear is fear itself," the president declared in his inaugural address to the nation.

In a certain sense, it is fair to say that the New Deal merely introduced types of social and economic reform that had been familiar to many Europeans for more than a generation. Moreover, the New Deal represented the culmination of a long-range trend toward abandonment of "laissez-faire" capitalism, going back to the regulation of the railroads in the 1880s, and the flood of state and national reform legislation introduced in the Progressive era of Theodore Roosevelt and Woodrow Wilson.

What was truly novel about the New Deal, however, was the speed with which it accomplished what previously had taken generations. In fact, many of the reforms were hastily drawn and weakly administered; some actually contradicted others. And during the entire New Deal era, public criticism and debate were never interrupted or suspended; in fact, the New Deal brought to the individual citizen a sharp revival of interest in government.

When Roosevelt took the presidential oath, the banking and credit system of the nation was in a state of paralysis. With astonishing rapidity the nation's banks were first closed – and then reopened only if they were solvent. The administration adopted a policy of moderate currency inflation to start an upward movement in commodity prices and to afford some relief to debtors. New governmental agencies brought generous credit facilities to industry and agriculture. The Federal Deposit Insurance Corporation (FDIC) insured savings-bank deposits up to $5,000, and severe regulations were imposed upon the sale of securities on the stock exchange.

Unemployment

By 1933, millions of Americans were out of work. Bread lines were a common sight in most cities. Hundreds of thousands roamed the country in search of food, work and shelter. "Brother, can you spare a dime?" went the refrain of a popular song.

An early step for the unemployed came in the form of the Civilian Conservation Corps (CCC), a program enacted by Congress to bring relief to young men between 18 and 25 years of age. Run in semi-military style, the CCC enrolled jobless young men in work camps across the country for about $30 per month. About 2 million young men took part during the decade. They participated in a variety of conservation projects: planting trees to combat soil erosion and maintain national forests; eliminating stream pollution; creating fish, game and bird sanctuaries; and conserving coal, petroleum, shale, gas, sodium and helium deposits.

Work relief came in the form of the Civil Works Administration. Although criticized as "make work", the jobs funded ranged from ditch digging to highway repairs to teaching. Created in November 1933, it was abandoned in the spring of 1934. Roosevelt and his key officials, however, continued to favor unemployment programs based on work relief rather than welfare.

Agriculture

The New Deal years were characterized by a belief that greater regulation would solve many of the country's problems. In 1933, for example, Congress passed the Agricultural Adjustment Act (AAA) to provide economic relief to farmers. The AAA had at its core a plan to raise crop prices by paying farmers a subsidy to compensate for voluntary cutbacks in production. Funds for the payments would be generated by a tax levied on industries that processed crops. By the time the act had become law, however, the growing season was well underway, and the AAA encouraged farmers to plow under their abundant crops. Secretary of Agriculture Henry A. Wallace called this activity a "shocking commentary on our civilization." Nevertheless, through the AAA and the Commodity Credit Corporation, a program which extended loans for crops kept in storage and off the market, output dropped.

The Second New Deal

In its early years, the New Deal sponsored a remarkable series of legislative initiatives and achieved significant increases in production and prices – but it did not bring an end to the Depression. And as the sense of immediate crisis eased, new demands emerged. Businessmen mourned the end of "laissez-faire" and chafed under the regulations of the NIRA. Vocal attacks also mounted from the political left and right as dreamers, schemers and politicians alike emerged with economic panaceas that drew wide audiences of those dissatisfied with the pace of recovery.

In the face of these pressures from left and right, President Roosevelt backed a new set of economic and social measures. Prominent among these were measures to fight poverty, to counter unemployment with work and to provide a social safety net.

The Works Progress Administration (WPA), the principal relief agency of the so-called second New Deal, was an attempt to provide work rather than welfare. Under the WPA, buildings, roads, airports and schools were constructed. Actors, painters, musicians and writers were employed through the Federal Theater Project, the Federal Art Project and the Federal Writers Project. In addition, the National Youth Administration gave part-time employment to students, established training programs and provided aid to unemployed youth. The WPA only included about three million jobless at a time; when it was abandoned in 1943 it had helped a total of 9 million people. From 1932 to 1938, there was widespread public debate on the meaning of New Deal policies to the nation's political and economic life. It became obvious that Americans wanted the government to take greater responsibility for the welfare of the nation. Indeed, historians generally credit the New Deal with establishing the foundations of the modern welfare state in the United States. Some New Deal critics argued that the indefinite extension of government functions would eventually undermine the liberties of the people. But President Roosevelt insisted that measures fostering economic well-being would strengthen liberty and democracy.

In a radio address in 1938, Roosevelt reminded the American people that:

Democracy has disappeared in several other great nations, not because the people of those nations disliked democracy, but because they had grown tired of unemployment and insecurity, of seeing their children hungry while they sat helpless in the face of government confusion and government weakness through lack of leadership … Finally, in desperation,

they chose to sacrifice liberty in the hope of getting something to eat. We in America know that our de-
215 mocratic institutions can be preserved and made to work. But in order to preserve them we need ... to prove that the practical operation of democratic government is equal to the task of protecting the secu-rity of the people ... The people of America are in agreement in defending their liberties at any cost, 220 and the first line of the defense lies in the protection of economic security.

from: http://www.english.uiuc.edu/maps/depression/overview.htm

1. Explain the developments that led to the Great Depression.

2. Why did the Depression quickly turn into a worldwide economic slump?

3. State the consequences for the political sphere.

4. Mention some of the measures that were introduced as part of the framework of the New Deal.

5. Explain the workings of the Agricultural Adjustment Act and its consequences.

6. List some of the measures of the Second New Deal, and explain the WPA in more detail.

7. Point out how President Roosevelt aimed to defend democracy.

In den sich anschließenden Stunden liegt der Schwerpunkt auf der inhaltlichen und stilistischen Analyse von zwei Zeitungsartikeln jeweils aus der Zeit der *Depression* und aus der heutigen aktuellen Krisenlage an der *Wall Street.* Die Hausaufgabe zu dieser Stunde besteht darin, den Leitartikel *(editorial)* „Relief, Today und Tomorrow" *(Copy 9)* von 1936 zu lesen und sprachlich vorzubereiten.

Am Anfang der nächsten Unterrichtsstunde sollte der Artikel im Unterricht laut vorgelesen werden. Da dieser Leitartikel vor über 70 Jahren geschrieben wurde, sind die sprachlichen Unterschiede zwischen beiden Artikeln ein weiterer interessanter Analyse-Aspekt. Die im *editorial* verwendete Sprache zeichnet sich im Gegensatz zu vielen heute geschriebenen Artikeln nicht durch *colloquialisms* oder Bezüge zu literarischen Werken aus, sondern erscheint etwas trockener und distanzierter.

Nachdem das Verständnis auf der sprachlichen Ebene gesichert wurde, wird der Inhalt kurz zusammengefasst. Dies kann in Form eines kurzen Unterrichtsgespräches geschehen.

> ### Sum up the contents of the editorial *Relief, Today and Tomorrow (Copy 9).*
>
> The editorial *Relief, Today and Tomorrow* was written before Roosevelt's second campaign for president. In it, the author voices his criticism of the advocates of the "balance the budget" – proposal, outlining this goal as unrealistic and remote. To corroborate his opinion, he gives some estimates about the number of unemployed people and people on federal, state or local relief. At that particular time (January 1936), about 5,000,000 people were being cared for by the state. A calculation is provided which shows that in the year 1936 3,500,000 families were receiving $850 which was about half the subsistence-level, and that 8,000,000 unemployed people were not receiving any support at all. The author moves on by stating that although the federal government is spending enormous sums of money, the people concerned are still suffering from deprivation. Moreover, the sums of money granted differ from state to state, for example, in the New England states, people can live quite decently on relief, whereas in the Southeastern states, this is not possible in any way. A reference is made to an article in the *Annalist* where general criticism of the over-costly federal relief program can be found and a return to the dole is suggested. The author's opinion is that this solution would offer many advantages, but that work relief is generally preferable to the dole. Finally, he refers to another magazine where the necessity of the same government expenditures, together with social-security legislation and increased taxation, has been advocated by people in charge of national organizations, stating that no change in the economic and social situation is in sight.

Im nächsten Schritt wird eine Analyse im stilistischen Bereich durchgeführt, um herauszuarbeiten, mit welchen Mitteln der Autor vorgeht, um seine Haltung zu den Kritikern des *relief program* zu untermauern.

Diese Aufgabe kann am besten in Gruppenarbeit bearbeitet werden. Dabei bekommt jede Gruppe eine Folie mit dem unten angegebenen Raster, um ihre jeweiligen Ergebnisse einzutragen. Anschließend werden die Folien zusammen auf dem OHP präsentiert, sodass eine möglichst vollständige Darstellung der Stilmittel erreicht wird.

Editorial: Relief, Today and Tomorrow

relief money, food, or other help given to those in poverty or need

"BALANCE the budget" is the war cry with which the anti-Administration forces will advance against Mr. Roosevelt in the coming campaign. In the words of the mellifluous Governor Talmadge, "Shall we continue to borrow and spend, or settle down and settle up?" Without the Georgia Governor's fireworks, even Governor Landon, in a discussion
5 of the unbalanced budget, declared that "relief appropriation has been more than ample," but that bureaucracy has taken more than its share of the amount that should have been spent on the unemployed.

mellifluous sweetly or smoothly flowing; here: eloquent

appropriation an act of legislature authorizing money to be paid from the treasury for a specified use

In the light of these criticisms, it is pertinent to inquire just how much the federal government is spending for relief, and how wide an area these appropriations are cov-
10 ering. Estimates of the number of unemployed in the country today vary from nine to seventeen million. The American Federation of Labor estimates 11,672,000 as of November, 1935. For the week ending January 4, 1936, there were approximately 3,550,000 persons on the federal work-relief pay roll. With the termination of the FERA approximately 1,500,000 unemployables were transferred from federal relief to state or local
15 aid. Assuming that all of these persons are now obtaining some form of government assistance, we have a total of a little over 5,000,000 being cared for today by the state, leaving, according to the A. F. of L., about 6,500,000 unemployed for whom no such provision is being made.

pertinent having precise or logical relevance to the matter at hand

FERA Federal Emergency Relief Association

Last spring an appropriation of $4,800,000,000 was made for federal relief: the eight
20 hundred million to be expended before the end of the fiscal year in June, 1935, the remainder to be used for relief in the current year. An article in the *Annalist* for January 24 estimates that something like a billion of this will be still unexpended on June 30 next. The annual expenditure for relief this year, therefore, will be almost the same as it was last, namely, three billion dollars. Assuming that every dollar of this sum is used
25 for direct relief of the unemployed, it means an expenditure of $850 a year each for 3,500,000 people; each of these, however, represents a family unit of three and a half persons. What it amounts to is that the federal government supports 3,500,000 families at $850 a year each, or about half the subsistence-level income as it is generally estimated, and that the remaining 8,000,000 unemployed – also presumably representing
30 families and not individuals – are dependent upon admittedly inadequate state or municipal relief, the casual benefits of private charity, or their own dwindling resources. From this standpoint it is seen that, although the federal government is spending enormous sums of money, it is hardly plunging the beneficiaries into luxury. Elsewhere in this issue Mr. Feinstein indicates what these expenditures mean when separated into
35 geographical and personal units. At best, in the New England states, where the relief rate is highest, they mean enough to eat, of a sort, shelter, and fuel, with almost no allowance for clothing or household necessities. At worst, in the Southeastern states, where the average monthly relief grant per family is $17.50, they mean something less. Yet even this meager allotment is considered extravagant by the advocates of a balanced
40 budget, and Mr. Roosevelt himself wishes to give the impression that some attempt will soon be made to scale down relief expenditures.
The *Annalist* article offers general criticism of the over-costly federal relief program, and suggests an alternative which may be taken as the program of many Administration critics. It is simply a return to the dole, as the least expensive way of meeting what is
45 admittedly a problem of large-scale distress. This would have the additional advantage of eliminating government competition with private industry, so objectionable to Mr. Smith's Liberty Leaguers. It is perfectly true that, as it is now administered, the work-relief program of the government is not all that could be desired. There is undeniably a good deal of boondoggling and extravagant overcrowding at the top. But when useful
50 work is economically performed, work relief is obviously preferable to the dole. In the

to expend (*fml.*) to spend

subsistence-level the level needed to cover basic survival needs such as food and shelter
dwindling becoming smaller and smaller

allotment a share granted

dole a form of social security payment to the unemployed

to boondoggle to do work of no or little practical value merely to keep or look busy

January *Survey* the directors of thirteen national organizations discussed relief now and in the future. None of them could see an immediate prospect of smaller government expenditures. Most of them thought, with the inevitable decline of private resources attendant upon six years of depression, that this would be the "worst winter yet". Al-
55 most without exception they called for a federal program that was definite and consistent and that at the same time recognized relief as a more or less permanent problem. Even with the return of "recovery", estimates of probable unemployment range from six to eight million. These recommendations are made by persons in direct, daily contact with the suffering and insecurity that unemployment brings. Without ad-
60 equate social-security legislation, based on increased taxation, proposals to "balance the budget" are bound to seem unrealistic and remote.

from: *The Nation*, February 12, 1936; http://newdeal.feri.org/texts/56.htm

attendant going along with; accompanying
consistent constantly adhering to the same principles, course or form

Work out the stylistic and rhetoric devices the author uses to point out 1. the dramatic situation of the unemployed and the socially deprived people and 2. his own opinion about the advocates of the balanced budget.

Mögliche Lösungen:

stylistic device	text	function
alliteration	Relief, **T**oday and **T**omorrow (headline)	• to emphasize the continued provision of relief services
alliteration	**B**alance the **b**udget (l. 1)	• to point out the issue of the supporters of a reduced relief budget
parallelism	how much the federal ... how wide an area ... (ll. 8 f.)	• to prepare the reader for a detailed analysis of the insufficiency of the relief budget
statistical data	The American Federation of Labor ... about 6,500,000 unemployed for whom no such provision is being made (l. 11 – l. 18)	• to support his opinion that relief payments are still inadequate
group of three	upon admittedly inadequate state ... or their own dwindling resources (ll. 30 ff.)	• to make the difficult situation of the families more memorable and resonant
exaggeration, irony	hardly plunging the beneficiaries into luxury (l. 33)	• to stress the inadequacy of the relief payments
understatement	It is perfectly true that, as it is now administered, ... is not all that could be desired. (ll. 47 f.)	• to discreetly voice some criticism about the existing work-relief program
antithesis	**At best**, in the New England states, ... **At worst**, in the Southeastern states, ... (ll. 35 ff.)	• to point out the difference in payments and their consequences
emphatic use	Almost without exception ... (ll. 54 f.)	• to draw the readers' attention to the unanimous demands of the directors

Anschließend wird der Zeitungsartikel *Wall Street's Masters of the Universe are dethroned (Copy 10)* analysiert.

Um einen besseren Eindruck von der in diesem Artikel verwendeten Sprache zu bekommen und als Kontrast zum vorherigen Artikel sollte er zunächst auch laut vorgelesen werden. Im nächsten Schritt wird er dann sprachlich und inhaltlich erarbeitet. Falls die Zeit nicht ausreicht, kann dies auch als Hausaufgabe aufgegeben werden.

In einem weiteren Schritt werden nun die Stilmittel herausgearbeitet, die der Autor benutzt, um die schockierte Stimmung an der Wall Street und in den USA und die durch das fahrlässige Verhalten der *investment banker* herbeigeführten dramatischen Konsequenzen zu beschreiben.

Wall Street's Masters of the Universe are dethroned

Ben Macintyre on Wall Street

Wall Street looks the same: the same sharp-suited brokers swinging the same mono-grammed attaché cases; the blue-jacketed traders smoking and gossiping outside the Stock Exchange; the same air of ambient wealth, gambling and nervous expectation.
5 Yet Wall Street has changed for ever, and everyone on it knows.

After the financial upheavals of the past few weeks, the voting-down of the bailout in Washington, the precipitous fall of the Dow on Monday, the landscape of the famous street looks very different. Yesterday a bulldozer was digging a large hole in front of the New York Stock Exchange: inside, the Earth has moved, too.

10 The change is partly structural, partly political and partly cultural. The five great invest-ments banks that dominated Wall Street, and world finance, are no more: two have failed, one is selling up to the Bank of America, and the others have become commer-cial banks. The era of the self-regarding, massively self-rewarding independent invest-ment banker, the financial colossus of the past few years, is over. "The world has
15 changed," a spokesman for Morgan Stanley declared last week. It is, William Isaac, former chairman of the Federal Deposit Insurance Corporation, which helps to guar-antee bank deposits, said, "the end of Wall Street as we have known it".

The centre of financial gravity has abruptly shifted to Washington. It is the legislators who now hold America's financial future in their hands. Those "Masters of the Uni-
20 verse" Tom Wolfe wrote about in *Bonfire of the Vanities* are now not even masters of Wall Street. Regulators are poised to bring the wild boys of the financial world to book, and to keep them reined in; the American public is determined that someone be made to pay.

But it may be the cultural shift that is most profound, and least easy to see. "Wall Street:
25 RIP," pronounced *The New York Times* last weekend. "A world of big egos. A world where people love to roll the dice with borrowed money, of tightwire trading, propelled by computers … that world is largely coming to an end."

You could see the change in the taut faces of the workers filing into the Stock Exchange yesterday morning: they might have been lining up for a particularly gruelling and
30 unpredictable exam. Most declined to speak.

The shift showed in little ways: at a coffee shop around the corner, one woman com-plained that her morning bagel was 20 cents more expensive than the day before. "It went up today? Already?" she exclaimed. "Bear Stearns, AIG, now my bagel . . ." she grumbled, a litany of economic woe.

35 Outside the shop, Rosario Catania was panhandling: "Done better than I expected," he said. "Numbers went down 700 yesterday, but picked up again this morning." On Wall Street, even the beggars are speculators.

Andrew Schlieman was walking an impossibly tiny dog, Kingston, outside the ex-change. "I got out two years ago," he said. "What's happening is the opposite of irra-
40 tional exuberance. It's the downside of capitalism, the opportunism and greed. It's the American way. Gordon Gekko said it best, 'Greed is good'," a reference to the character played by Michael Douglas in the film *Wall Street,* which showed the street's excesses at their most lurid, and most attractive.

For the past two decades, the Gordon Gekkos have been envied and criticised, but
45 often secretly admired, by the rest of America. Today they are loathed and vilified to a depth and with an intensity that has not been felt for 80 years. That fury vented itself, via Congress, with the rejection of the bailout Bill on Monday. Even if it hurts them, Americans want to hurt the people who got rich and made America ill on toxic credit.

50 "This is the most lucrative business on the planet, but there's a right way to do it and wrong way," Jim Foster, a broker at Gotham Realty Holdings, said. "The market will come back – in three, maybe four years …" That sentiment was widely expressed by

broker agent who buys or sells for a client on a commission basis, with-out having title to the property bought or sold
ambient encompassing
bailout giving money to a company, country, etc. that has serious financial difficulties
precipitous abrupt

investment bank a financial institution that deals chiefly in the underwriting of new securities

gravity the force that at-tracts different objects in space towards each other

to rein in to control and direct as if by reins like a horse

RIP *Requiescat in pace.* From Latin: May he/she rest in peace

Stock Exchange an asso-ciation of brokers and dealers in stocks and bonds who meet to-gether and transact busi-ness according to fixed rules

to panhandle to sit down in a corner trying to look dejected and in need of money

lurid lit or shining with an unnatural, fiery glow

toxic poisonous

Wall Street workers yesterday, but without the optimism and conviction that is characteristic of Wall Street, and vital to its success.

55 That is what has changed most fundamentally. The writer and economist John Kenneth Galbraith identified the essential ingredient of financial feelgood: "Speculation on a large scale requires a pervasive sense of confidence and optimism and conviction that ordinary people were meant to be rich … Such a feeling of trust is essential for a boom. When people are cautious, questioning, misanthropic, suspicious, or mean, they are 60 immune to speculative enthusiasms."

Enthusiasm was gone from Wall Street yesterday, replaced by a febrile uncertainty and a foreboding that 2008 might turn into 1929. Most economists do not believe that a Thirties-style Depression is in the offing. America's irrepressible financial gamblers will find another way to make quick, huge money, and buy a bigger yacht. The earth will 65 stop moving under Wall Street, and the bulldozer will leave. But as the tourists, brokers and traders look up at the ledges high above Wall Street, they are all wondering the same thing.

In fact there were only two suicide jumps related to the Crash of 1929 and tales of mass suicide became fact, based on rumour, fear and uncertainty. That, as the world has just 70 seen, is how Wall Street works.

from: *The Times,* october 1, 2008; http://business.timesonline.co.uk/tol/business/markets/article4856942.ece

misanthropic unfriendly or morose

febrile feverish

in the offing at a distance, but within sight

Sum up the contents of the article in a few sentences.

Work out the stylistic and rhetoric devices the author uses to point out the dramatic impact of the current situation and the brokers' lack of willingness to take on responsibility.
Find evidence in the article about the author's attitude towards the actions of the investment bankers.

Diese Aufgabe kann, wie oben schon beschrieben, wiederum in Gruppenarbeit bearbeitet werden. Dabei bekommt jede Gruppe eine Folie mit dem unten angegebenen Raster, um ihre jeweiligen Ergebnisse einzutragen. Anschließend werden die Folien wieder zusammen auf dem OHP präsentiert, sodass eine möglichst vollständige Darstellung der Stilmittel erreicht wird.

Mögliche Lösungen:

stylistic device	text	function
alliteration	same sharp-suited brokers swinging the same ... (l. 2)	• to emphasize the professional outward appearance of the brokers
antithesis	Wall Street **looks the same:** ... Yet Wall Street **has changed for ever**, ... (l. 2; l. 5)	• to point out the enormity of the change that has occured
"change" used as a leitmotif	has changed (l. 5); change (l. 10); "The World has changed", (ll. 14f.); change (l. 28)	• to point out that a new era has started and to even more emphasize it by constantly referring to it
landscape-metaphor	precipitous fall of the Dow (l. 7), the landscape of the famous streets (ll. 7f.), a bulldozer was digging a large hole ... (ll. 8f.), the Earth has moved ... (l. 9)	• to appeal to the reader's imagination: the near-crash as an enormous shock changing the earth's surface
allusion to "The New Colossus" (Emma Lazarus)	the financial colossus of the past few years ... (ll. 14f.)	• to make a connection between the Statue of Liberty standing for the fulfillment of the AD and the investment bankers' interpretation of it
quotations from several people	William Isaac, ... said, "the end of Wall Street as we have known it". (ll. 15–17); Andrew Schlieman ... "I got out two years ago," he said. "What's happening is the opposite of irrational exuberance. It's the downside of capitalism, the opportunism and greed. It's the American way. Gordon Gekko said it best, 'Greed is good', ... (l. 38 – l. 43)	• to attribute more reliability to the previously given assessment of the situation and to highlight the negative consequences of capitalism

stylistic device	text	function
quotation from the *The New York Times*	"Wall Street: RIP," pronounced *The New York Times* last weekend. "A world of big egos. A world where people love to roll the dice with borrowed money, of tightwire trading, propelled by computers … that world is largely coming to an end." (l. 24 – l. 27)	• to express a critical view on the ongoing events by referring to a prestigious newspaper
repetition	Even if it hurts them, Americans want to hurt the people who got rich and made America ill on toxic credit. (ll. 47 ff.)	• to emphasize the attitude of the Americans towards the bankers' actions
contrast	**For the past two decades**, the Gordon Gekkos have been envied and criticised, but often secretly admired, by the rest of America. **Today** they are loathed and vilified to a depth and with an intensity that has not been felt for 80 years. (ll. 44 ff.)	• to point out the changed attitude of the Americans towards the dealings of the brokers, showing an ever-present aspect of ambivalence
alliteration	**w**as **w**idely expressed by **W**all Street **w**orkers … (ll. 52 f.)	• to highlight the brokers' optimistic resolve to evaluate the consequences of the crisis
group of three	The change is partly structural, partly political and partly cultural. (l. 10)	• to make the idea more memorable and resonant
allusion to title of a famous novel	Wall Street's Masters of the Universe (headline)	• to imply a comparison with the politicians in the novel who also suffer from megalomania

The article not only states objective facts and developments, but also reflects the author's opinion on the events on Wall Street. The author criticizes the irresponsible dealings of the investment bankers not in a very open, but in a more subtle way. To this end, for example, he quotes some lines from an article from *The New York Times* that displays a very critical attitude towards what has happened ("A world of big egos. A world … that world is largely coming to an end."; ll. 25 ff.). Moreover, another former banker is quoted who also voices a censorious opinion on the events on Wall Street (Andrew Schlieman … "I got out two years ago," he said. "What's happening is the opposite of irrational exuberance. It's the downside of capitalism, the opportunism and greed. It's the American way. Gordon Gekko said it best, 'Greed is good'," …; l. 38 – l. 41). There is even an ironic note in the headline 'Wall Street's Masters of the Universe are dethroned' which already prepares the reader for a more complex discussion of the developments. Another point that implies a critical attitude on the author's part is the reference to the feelings of many Americans towards the brokers and their actions, which are described in drastic words ("Today they are loathed and vilified to a depth … people who got rich and made America ill on toxic credit"; l. 45 – l. 49). Very appropriately, the article ends with an allegory about the workings of Wall Street, by making a connection with the alleged number of suicides after the Crash of 1929 and referring to the importance of rumour, fear and uncertainty in both cases.

In diesem Zusammenhang erscheint eine Diskussion über den wirtschaftlichen Hintergrund angesichts der aktuellen Entwicklungen auf dem Aktienmarkt angemessen. Dazu ist es notwendig, sich zunächst über die beiden unterschiedlichen ökonomischen Ansätze zu informieren, die zum Beispiel in Deutschland praktizierte soziale Marktwirtschaft *(social market economy),* die staatliche Regulierung bis zu einem gewissen Maß erlaubt, und das gänzlich freie Spiel der Kräfte ohne staatliche Intervention *(free market without state intervention).* Zudem ist es notwendig, dass die Schülerinnen und Schüler Kenntnisse über das Entstehen der Immobilienkrise in den USA und den Weiterverkauf von Kreditpaketen an europäische Banken gewinnen. Weiterhin sollten einige der Möglichkeiten genannt werden (Aktienpakete, Optionsscheine, usw.), mit denen Investment-Banker diese enormen Gewinne machen konnten. Natürlich ist eine solche Diskussion, was den fachlichen Hintergrund angeht, nur auf einer oberflächlichen Basis möglich, da die entsprechenden Kenntnisse über Vorgänge im Bankenwesen nicht vorhanden sein können.

Die Diskussion sollte auch die Ära der *Great Depression* mit einbeziehen. 1929 haben ähnliche überhitzte Entwicklungen auf dem Aktienmarkt zum Börsencrash geführt, der dann die Ära der *Great Depression* eingeleitet hat, die durch hohe Arbeitslosigkeit und Verelendung ganzer Bevölkerungsschichten gekennzeichnet war. Zudem ist es auch wichtig, den *New Deal* und seine damaligen Auswirkungen auf die amerikanische Gesellschaft zu beleuchten. In diesem Zusammenhang kann auf den ersten Artikel eingegangen werden, der die soziale Unterstützung des Staates propagiert, jedoch für noch nicht ausreichend hält.

Es erscheint nicht sinnvoll, eine Diskussion herbeizuführen, die kontrovers von Vertretern der Positionen der unterschiedlichen Wirtschaftssysteme geführt werden soll, weil das ökonomische Hintergrundwissen nicht vorhanden ist. Jedoch ist es erstrebenswert, die in diesem Themenkomplex auftretenden ökonomischen Wirkungsweisen einmal in einer auch für Schülerinnen und Schüler verständlichen Weise zu beleuchten und zu besprechen.

Try to find out some reasons why the stock market on Wall Street has come close to crashing and look at the role the investment bankers have played (e.g. developments in the American real estate market, dealing with stock purchase warrants and other stock market products). Draw some comparisons with the time after the Crash in 1929 and take into consideration the ensuing developments in the USA in the economic and social sectors and the effects of the "New Deal".

Maycomb's points of view

In *Component 2* geht es nach der inhaltlichen Klärung der Ereignisse, die in den Kapiteln 12 bis 19 beschrieben werden, um die Analyse der Erzählperspektive des Romans. Dabei sollen den Schülerinnen und Schülern auch grundlegende Aspekte der wichtigsten in der Literatur verwendeten *points of view* (wie sie wahrscheinlich in der Jahrgangsstufe 11 eingeführt worden sind) in Erinnerung gebracht werden.

Anschließend liegt der Schwerpunkt des Unterrichts auf der Untersuchung des Aspekts Rassismus, wie er sich in der Haltung der Figuren zur Übernahme der Verteidigung des schwarzen Angeklagten Tom Robinson durch den weißen Anwalt Atticus, zum Verbrechen, zur Rassenmischung sowie in der räumlichen Trennung von Schwarz und Weiß in Maycomb manifestiert.

Dazu werden relevante Passagen des Romans und auch des Films bearbeitet.

Der Einstieg in die Stunde erfolgt über die in Hausarbeit geleistete Vokabelarbeit *(Copy 11)*. Die Ergebnisse werden für alle gesichert, indem ein Schüler entweder eine Definition vorliest und ein anderer Schüler das entsprechende Wort nennt oder umgekehrt, indem ein Schüler ein Wort nennt und ein anderer Schüler die passende Definition vorliest.

Lösungen zu Copy 11:

Chapter 12:	
values	**8** [plural] your ideas about what is right and wrong, or what is important in life
slave	**18** someone who is owned by another person and works for them for no money
curiosity	**3** [singular, uncountable] the desire to know about something
uncompromising	**16** unwilling to change your opinions, ideas or intentions
Chapter 13:	
influence	**32** the power to affect the way someone or something develops, behaves, or thinks without using direct force or orders
to ignore	**22** to deliberately pay no attention to something that you have been told or that you know about
tactful	**27** avoiding saying things that are likely to upset or embarrass other people
dump	**9** a place where unwanted waste is taken and left
Chapter 14:	
to apologize	**25** to tell someone that you are sorry that you have done something wrong
unbearable	**2** too unpleasant, painful, or annoying to deal with
darkness	**23** when there is no light
mean (adj.)	**13** cruel or not kind

Chapter 15:	
nightmare	**6** a very difficult, unpleasant, or frightening dream, experience or situation
trial	**33** a legal process in which a judge and often a jury examine information in a court of law to decide whether someone is guilty of a crime
mob	**12** a large noisy crowd, especially one that is angry and violent
polite	**14** behaving or speaking in a way that is seen as correct for the social situation you are in, and considerate of others
Chapter 16:	
to despise	**20** to dislike and have a low opinion of someone or something
human (adj.)	**28** belonging to or relating to people, especially as opposed to machines or animals
to testify	**30** to make a formal statement of what is true, especially in a court of law
drugstore	**5** a shop where you can buy medicines, beauty products, etc.
Chapter 17:	
to identify	**17** to recognize and correctly name someone or something
injury	**21** a wound or other damage to part of your body caused by an accident or attack
to corroborate	**1** to provide information that supports or helps to prove someone else's statement, ideas, etc.
filthy	**24** very dirty
ambidextrous	**15** able to use either hand equally well
Chapter 18:	
fragile	**4** easily broken or damaged [= delicate; ≠ strong]
prejudice	**10** an unreasonable dislike and distrust of people who are different from you in some way, especially because of their race, sex, religion, etc. – used to show disapproval
hostility	**31** unfriendliness and anger towards another person
compassion	**29** a strong feeling of sympathy for someone who is suffering, and a desire to help them
Chapter 19:	
nickel	**26** a coin in the US or Canada that is worth five cents
decent	**7** following moral standards that are acceptable to society
guilt	**19** a strong feeling of shame and sadness because you know that you have done something wrong
impudent	**11** rude and showing no respect for other people

Dann wird in einem Unterrichtsgespräch die inhaltliche Entwicklung, wie sie in den Kapiteln 12 bis 19 dargestellt wird, anhand der *while-reading tasks (Copy 12)* geklärt, die die Schüler auch in vorbereitender Hausarbeit lösen können.

While-reading chapters 12–19

Find the corresponding definitions for the words.

Chapter 12:	
values	**1** to provide information that supports or helps to prove someone else's statement, ideas, etc.
slave	**2** too unpleasant, painful, or annoying to deal with
curiosity	**3** [singular, uncountable] the desire to know about something
uncompromising	**4** easily broken or damaged [= delicate; ≠ strong]
Chapter 13:	
influence	**5** a shop where you can buy medicines, beauty products, etc.
to ignore	**6** a very difficult, unpleasant, or frightening dream, experience or situation
tactful	**7** following moral standards that are acceptable to society
dump	**8** [plural]: your ideas about what is right and wrong, or what is important in life
Chapter 14:	
to apologize	**9** a place where unwanted waste is taken and left
unbearable	**10** an unreasonable dislike and distrust of people who are different from you in some way, especially because of their race, sex, religion, etc. – used to show disapproval
darkness	**11** rude and showing no respect for other people
mean (adj.)	**12** a large noisy crowd, especially one that is angry and violent
Chapter 15:	
nightmare	**13** cruel or not kind
trial	**14** behaving or speaking in a way that is seen as correct for the social situation you are in and considerate of others
mob	**15** able to use either hand equally well
polite	**16** unwilling to change your opinions, ideas or intentions
Chapter 16:	
to despise	**17** to recognize and correctly name someone or something
human (adj.)	**18** someone who is owned by another person and works for them for no money
to testify	**19** a strong feeling of shame and sadness because you know that you have done something wrong
drugstore	**20** to dislike and have a low opinion of someone or something
Chapter 17:	
to identify	**21** a wound or other damage to part of your body caused by an accident or attack
injury	**22** to deliberately pay no attention to something that you have been told or that you know about
to corroborate	**23** when there is no light
filthy	**24** very dirty
ambidextrous	**25** to tell someone that you are sorry that you have done something wrong
Chapter 18:	
fragile	**26** a coin in the US or Canada that is worth five cents
prejudice	**27** avoiding saying things that are likely to upset or embarrass other people
hostility	**28** belonging to or relating to people, especially as opposed to machines or animals
compassion	**29** a strong feeling of sympathy for someone who is suffering, and a desire to help them
Chapter 19:	
nickel	**30** to make a formal statement of what is true, especially in a court of law
decent	**31** unfriendliness and anger towards another person
guilt	**32** the power to affect the way someone er something develops, behaves, or thinks without using direct force or orders
impudent	**33** a legal process in which a judge and often a jury examine information in a court of law to decide whether someone is guilty of a crime

While-reading tasks: chapters 12 – 19

While reading chapters 12 – 19, decide whether the following statements are true or false. Correct the false statements and indicate the page(s) and line(s) where you found the answer.

Chapter 12:
1. Calpurnia tells Scout to come into the kitchen when she wants to learn how to make bread.
2. When Jem and Scout walk into the black church with Calpurnia, people react in a respectful way.
3. Getting hymn-books for the First Purchase Church would not be very helpful because the members of the church community do not like singing.

Chapter 13:
1. Scout is happy about her aunt staying with them because she misses her mum.
2. Aunt Alexandra shares the views on the world with the people of Maycomb.

Chapter 14:
1. Atticus and Aunt Alexandra agree on Calpurnia's importance for the Finch family.
2. Scout gets furious at Jem because he does not let her read his books.
3. Dill has run away from his home because he feels unwanted.

Chapter 15:
1. Heck Tate is afraid there will be trouble because Tom Robinson is to be brought to the county jail in Maycomb.
2. On Sunday night, Atticus sits in front of the Maycomb jail because he wants to read his newspaper without Jem and Scout bothering him.
3. Scout talks to Mr Cunningham because she is scared of the mob and wants to help her father.

Chapter 16:
1. On the day of the trial, only a few white people have come to the courthouse in Maycomb.
2. Jem and Scout learn that the court had appointed Atticus to defend Tom Robinson.

Chapter 17:
1. Heck Tate testifies that Mayella's right eye was bruised.
2. There are nine children in the Ewell family.
3. Atticus reveals that Mr Ewell is left-handed.

Chapter 18:
1. When Mayella Ewell is in the witness stand, she gives evidence that she was on her back porch when she asked Sam Robinson to help her move a cupboard on the evening of November 21st.
2. Mrs Ewell died four years ago.
3. Mr Ewell is a heavy drinker.

Chapter 19:
1. On the evening of November 21st, the Ewell children were not at home because they had gone to the movies.
2. Tom Robinson tried to kiss Mayella, but she pushed him back and when Mr Ewell appeared at the window, Tom ran off.
3. During the cross-examination of Tom by Mr Gilmer, Dill starts crying because he is upset by the hateful behaviour of Mr Gilmor towards Tom Robinson.

Lösungen zu Copy 12:

Chapter 12:
1. False. Calpurnia tells Scouts to come into the kitchen when she feels lonely because Jem does not want to play with her. (p. 154, ll. 1–4)
2. True. (p. 157, l. 32–p. 158, l. 5)
3. False. Because they cannot read. (p. 165, l. 16)

Chapter 13:
1. False. Scout feels uncomfortable with her aunt because they don't have anything to talk about. Furthermore, she thinks her aunt does not like her (p. 170, ll. 18ff.) and that she is very different from her and Jem (p. 175, ll. 23–28)
2. True. (p. 174, l. 15–p. 175, l. 28)

Chapter 14:
1. False. Aunt Alexandra wants Calpurnia to leave the house, whereas Atticus considers her an important member of the family. He appreciates Calpurnia's style of educating his children. (p. 182, l. 25–p. 183, l. 2)
2. False. Scout gets furious at Jem because he tells her what to do (p. 184, ll. 9ff.) and because he tries to teach her.
3. True. (p. 190, ll. 19f.)

Chapter 15:
1. True. (p. 194, ll. 7ff.)
2. False. Atticus sits in front of the Maycomb jail because he fears that people will want to lynch Tom Robinson, and he wants to protect him. (p. 202, ll. 8ff.)
3. False. Scout talks to Mr Cunningham because she is not aware of the dangerous situation. She simply wants to be friendly and polite. (p. 204, l. 25–p. 206, l. 7)

Chapter 16:
1. False. A lot of white and black people have come to the courthouse, but they sit separately from each other. (p. 214, ll. 4ff.)
2. True. (p. 218, ll. 11f.)

Chapter 17:
1. True. (p. 225, ll. 12f.)
2. False. People do not know. Some think there are six children; others say there are nine children. (p. 228, ll. 23f.)
3. True. (p. 237, l. 23)

Chapter 18:
1. False. She was on the front porch when she asked Tom Robinson to help her to bust up a chiffarobe. (p. 240, l. 2)
2. False. Mayella says she does not remember when her mother died. (p. 244, l. 14)
3. True. (p. 244, ll. 27f.)

Chapter 19:
1. False. They had gone to town to buy ice creams. (p. 258, ll. 22f.)
2. False. Mayella tried to kiss him (p. 260, ll. 2–10)
3. True. (p. 265, ll. 21ff.)

2.1 See the other person's point of view

Zur allgemeinen Wiederholung der am häufigsten gebrauchten Erzählperspektiven und zur Vorbereitung der Analyse der Erzählperspektive in *To Kill a Mockingbird* führt die Lehrperson in einem kurzen Unterrichtsgespräch mit der Frage nach dem Unterschied zwischen *author* und *narrator* zum Thema hin.

> Whenever an author tells a story, there must be a storyteller (narrator). The storyteller is not identical with the author; rather the author chooses a narrator who can tell the story from different angles, i.e. points of view. The point of view establishes the relationship between the reader and the text.

Dann werden die zuvor in der jeweiligen Kursstärke entsprechend für Gruppen von vier Personen kopierten und in die einzelnen Abschnitte zerschnittenen *Copies 13, 14* und *15* verteilt, sodass jeder Kursteilnehmer einen Zettel erhält. Auf den *Copies* ist für die drei wichtigsten *points of view* Folgendes zu finden:
1. der Fachbegriff,
2. eine Erläuterung des Fachbegriffs,
3. eine Illustration des Fachbegriffs,
4. ein Beispiel aus der Literatur (Romanauszug).
Es gehören also je vier Schüler zusammen, die sich durch Umhergehen im Klassenraum und gegenseitiges Fragen finden sollen. Anschließend präsentiert je eine Gruppe pro Erzählperspektive ihr Ergebnis im Plenum.
Im nächsten Schritt sollen die Schülerinnen und Schüler ihr so reaktiviertes Wissen zur Erzählperspektive auf die Passage in Kapitel 14 anwenden, in der Atticus mit seiner Schwester Alexandra die Stellung Calpurnias in der Familie diskutiert (S. 181, Z. 9–32). Auch diese Ereignisse werden aus Scouts Sicht geschildert. An einigen Stellen wird die begrenzte Perspektive sehr deutlich, da sie ihre eigenen Empfindungen und Gedanken preisgibt, die Gefühle und Gedanken der anderen Personen aber nur indirekt wiedergibt, indem sie erzählt, was die Personen tun. Die Ich-Erzählerin Scout stellt sich auch selbst Fragen, sodass sich der Leser leicht in ihre Lage versetzen kann. In Partnerarbeit werden folgende Aufgaben gelöst:

> Scan the text (p. 181, ll. 9–32) for passages that indicate the *point of view* applied by the narrator, then explain it and point out the effect it has on the reader. Work with a partner and use a chart.

page, line	text	explanation	effect
p. 181, ll. 9 f.	"I told him in detail about our trip to church with Calpurnia."	The use of the personal pronoun "I" indicates the first-person narrator.	The reader knows that the narration is being told from a personal, individual point-of-view.
p. 181, ll. 10–12	"Atticus seemed to enjoy it, but Aunt Alexandra, who was sitting in a corner quietly sewing, put down her embroidery and stared at us."	Scout describes Atticus's and her aunt's reaction through her eyes. The reader does not know if Atticus really enjoyed it or why Alexandra stared at them. The narrator's point of view is limited to her own experiences.	The reader only learns what Scout thinks Atticus and her Aunt feel. So he/she will identify with the first-person narrator and see the scene through her eyes. The reader will perceive Atticus as likeable, Aunt Alexandra as hostile.

Point of View: First-person narrator

The first-person narrator is a character inside the story. He/she refers to himself/ herself as "I". He/she can only inform about what he/she knows feels, thinks and experiences. The point of view is limited to his/her experiences. The narrator can be either a main character or a minor character in the story. Because of the narrator's direct reporting of anything that happens, the reader feels as close to the protagonist as the narrator does. It is easy for the reader to identify with the narrator because he/she learns about the events just as the narrator does.

The first-person narrator lends the story credibility, authenticity and immediacy.

Ahead of me there's a body lying on the sidewalk. People walk around it, look down, keep going. I see their faces coming towards me bearing that careful rearrangement of the features that's meant to say, *This is none of my business.* When I get up even, I see that this person is a woman. She's lying on her back, staring straight at me. "Lady," she says. "Lady. Lady."

That word has been through lot. Noble lady, Dark lady, she's a real lady, old-lady lace, Listen lady, Hey lady watch where you're going, Ladies' Room, run through with lipstick and replaced with Women. But still the final word of appeal. If you want something very badly you do not say *Woman, Woman,* you say *Lady, Lady.* And she is saying that now.

I think *What if she's had a heart attack?* I look: there's blood on her forehead, not much, but a cut.

from: Margaret Atwood: *Cat's Eye.* London: Bloomsbury Publishing.

Point of view: Third-person narrator (selective-omniscient narrator)

The third-person narrator presents things as they are seen through the eyes of one or several characters in the story. The narrator himself/herself is not involved in the story and chooses to describe the thoughts and emotions of only one or several characters. The reader does not feel very close to the protagonists because the narrator tells the story in the third-person. He/she refers to the characters as "he/she/they …" He/she can only identify with those acting people to whose consciousness the perspective is limited, whose minds are explained by the narrator.

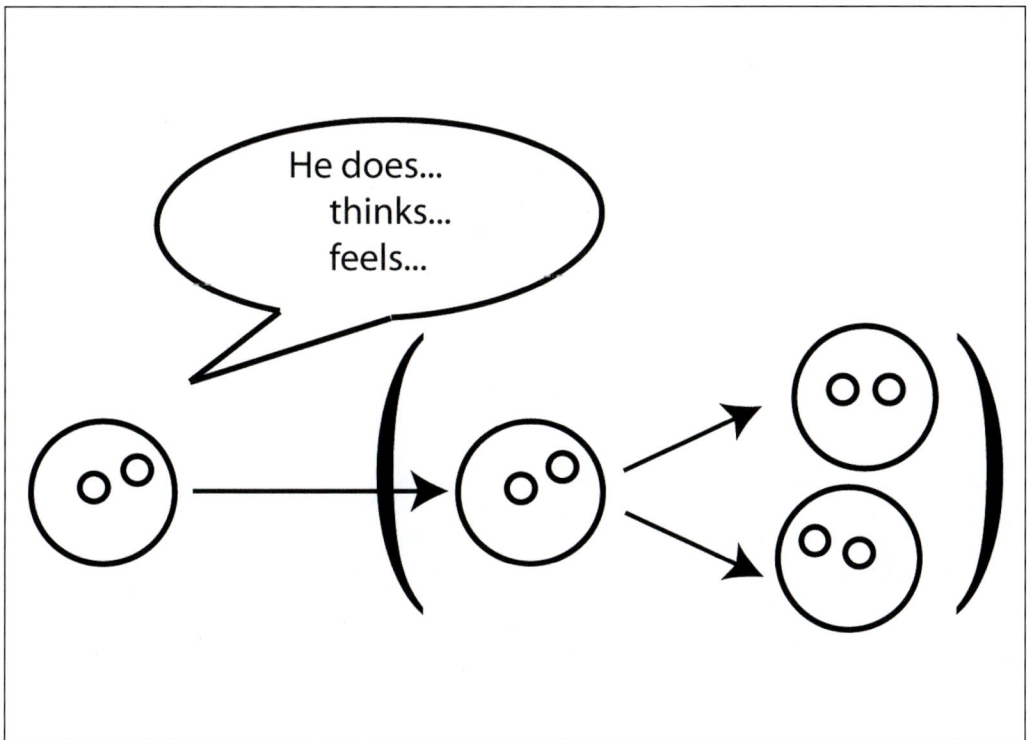

To his shame, Delaney's first thought was for the car (was it marred, scratched, dented?) and then for his insurance rates (what was this going to do to his good-driver discount?), and finally, belatedly, for the victim. Who was he? Where had he gone? Was he all right? Was he hurt? Bleeding? Dying? Delaney's hands trembled on the wheel. He reached mechanically for the key and choked off the radio. It was then, still strapped in and rushing with adrenaline, that the reality of it began to hit him: he'd injured, possibly killed, another human being. It wasn't his fault, god knew – the man was obviously insane, demented, suicidal, no jury would convict him – but there it was, all the same. Heart pounding, he slipped out from under the seat belt, eased open the door and stepped tentatively onto the parched strip of naked stone and litter that constituted the shoulder of the road.

from THE TORTILLA CURTAIN by T. Coraghessan Boyle, copyright © 1995 by T. Coraghessan Boyle. Used by permission of Viking Penguin, a division of Penguin Group (USA) Inc.

Point of view: Third-person narrator (omniscient narrator)

An omniscient narrator can move freely in time and space. He/she has an unlimited point of view, but does not participate in the action. He/she can shift from character to character, reporting what he/she chooses of their speech, actions, thoughts, feelings and emotions. He/she may give comments or decide to show the action without judgement. This perspective enables the narrator to know everything and to enter the minds of all the characters. The reader can easily identify with the acting persons, but he/she does not feel as directly spoken to as when a first-person narrator tells a story.

He had seen, for the very first time in his life, the face of a girl whose cheeks were not the colour of chocolate or dog-skin, whose hair was auburn and permanently waved, and whose expression (amazing novelty!) was one of benevolent interest. Lenina was smiling at him; such a nice-looking boy, she was thinking, and a really beautiful body. The blood rushed up into the young man's face; he dropped his eyes, raised them again for a moment only to find her still smiling at him, and was so much overcome that he had to turn away and pretend to be looking very hard at something on the other side of the square.

Bernard's questions made a diversion. Who? How? When? From where? Keeping his eyes fixed on Bernard's face (for so passionately did he long to see Lenina smiling that he simply dared not look at her), the young man tried to explain himself.

from: Aldous Huxley: *Brave New World*. © 1932 Mrs. Laura Huxley. Used by permission of Georges Borchardt Inc. Lit. Agency, New York (USA)

page, line	text	explanation	effect
p. 181, ll. 29–32	Atticus turned his head and spinned me to the wall with his good eye. His voice was deadly: 'First, apologize to your aunt.' 'Im sorry, Aunty,' I muttered.	The first-person narrator is a character in the story.	The reader feels involved in the story.
p. 182, ll. 4–7	"I understood, pondered a while, and concluded that the only way I could retire with a shred of dignity was to go to the bathroom, where I stayed long enough to make them think I had to go."	The first-person narrator tells the reader openly what she thinks and feels at that moment.	The reader can identify easily with Scout. She arouses his/her sympathy.
p. 182, l. 17	"Who was the 'her' they were talking about?"	The first-person narrator asks herself (and the reader) a question.	The reader will sympathize with the first-person narrator.

Um die Wirkung besser nachvollziehen zu können, die eine bestimmte Erzählperspektive auf den Leser und dessen Beziehung zum Text ausübt, schreiben die Schüler diesen Teil der Geschichte nun um. Gruppe 1 erzählt die Ereignisse aus der Sicht eines *third-person narrators, limited point of view* (und zwar aus der Sicht Alexandras). Gruppe 2 wählt einen *omniscient third-person narrator.* Während der anschließenden Präsentation machen die Zuhörer sich Notizen zu den unterschiedlichen Wirkungen auf den Leser.

Group 1: Rewrite the passage from *To Kill a Mockingbird* (p. 181, ll. 8–33). Use a third-person narrator perspective, telling the story from Aunt Alexandra's point of view.

Group 2: Rewrite the passage *To Kill a Mockingbird* (p. 181, ll. 8–33). Use an omniscient third-person narrator.

Die umgeschriebenen Texte könnten folgendermaßen aussehen:

Group 1: The passage told by a third-person narrator who describes the events from Aunt Alexandra's point of view.

Scout told Atticus about their trip to church with Calpurnia. He seemed to enjoy it, but Aunt Alexandra, who was sitting in a corner quietly sewing, was alarmed by the story. She put down her embroidery and stared at them.
"You all were coming back from Calpurnia's church that Sunday?"
Jem said: "Yessum, she took us."
Scout told Atticus that Calpurnia had invited her and Jem to come to her house some afternoon and she asked if they could go next Sunday. Aunt Alexandra was convinced that it was not good for the children to get so close to black people and so she got really upset by Scout's wish and said

63

vehemently: "You may not." Scout's reaction was very impolite. She wheeled around and said: "I didn't ask you!" Aunt Alexandra felt deeply offended by this rudeness. She had only wanted to protect the kids. She thought that Atticus was raising his children far too liberally.

He did not share his sister's opinion on black people, but he wanted to teach his kids to respect their aunt. That's why he made Scout apologize to her.

"I'm sorry, Aunty," she muttered.

Group 2: The passage told by an omniscient third-person narrator.

Scout told Atticus about their trip to Calpurnia's church. He actually enjoyed it because it made him feel proud of his unprejudiced children. Aunt Alexandra, who was sitting in a corner quietly sewing, however, was alarmed by the story. She put down her embroidery and stared at them.

"You were all coming back from Calpurnia's church that Sunday?" Jem said with a touch of pride: "Yessum, she took us."

Scout told Atticus excitedly that Calpurnia had invited her and Jem to come to her house some afternoon and asked if they could go next Sunday. She was sure that he would agree. But before Atticus could give a positive answer, Aunt Alexandra said very sharply "You may not." Aunt Alexandra shared Maycomb's attitude that white people should not mix with black people. Scout just couldn't understand why they shouldn't be allowed to go. She was so disappointed that she answered in a very impolite way, "I didn't ask you!"

She was surprised to see Atticus get up and down from his chair really fast. He was on his feet, upset. "Apologize to your aunt," he said. It was important for him to teach his children respect and politeness.

Since he insisted on her apology, Scout did him the favour and muttered "I'm sorry, Aunty."

Die Schülerinnen und Schüler werden beim Zuhören bemerkt haben, dass sich mit dem *point of view* die Sympathien verschieben, die der Leser für die einzelnen Figuren entwickelt.

While listening to the new versions, take notes on the effect the different *points of view* have on the reader.

Version 1 (Third-person narrator, selective omniscient, Aunt Alexandra's perspective):
Since the reader gets to know Aunt Alexandra's feelings and thoughts (and does not learn about Scout's emotions), Aunt Alexandra appears as a warmer, more caring person. The reader will understand her attitude better and thus perceive her as a kinder person.

Version 2 (Third-person omniscient narrator):
Since the narrator gives information on the feelings and thoughts of all the characters, he conveys a balanced picture and the reader will not side with one of the characters or be able to identify with him/her.

Zur Vertiefung des Themas besteht der erste Teil der Hausaufgabe darin, Atticus' Rat an seine Kinder, sich immer in die Lage des anderen zu versetzen, um ihn verstehen zu können, zu kommentieren.

Der zweite Teil der Hausaufgabe dient der Vorbereitung der nächsten Stunde. Die Lerngruppe informiert sich kurz über den Ku-Klux-Klan, der in Kapitel 15 (S. 196) erwähnt wird.

1. Comment on Atticus's advice to his children for getting along better with all kinds of people: "You never really understand a person until you consider things from his point of view." (p. 39, ll. 26–29)

2. Find basic information on the Ku Klux Klan and be prepared to talk about it.

2.2 Would you like to stand in Tom Robinson's shoes?

Zu Beginn der Stunde erhalten die Schüler die Gelegenheit, die Informationen zum Ku-Klux-Klan dem Kurs mitzuteilen, indem jeder Schüler einen Satz dazu sagt und die Aussagen sich so zu einem runden Bild ergänzen, das die Schüler auf das Thema Rassismus einstimmt. Ein

Bild auf Folie oder an der Tafel befestigt kann die Informationen anschaulich unterstützen. Folgende Beschreibung des KKK wird sich in etwa ergeben:

The Ku Klux Klan is a secret American political organization of Protestant white men who oppose people of other races or religions. They are dedicated to the supremacy of White Americans and intimidate and terrorize Blacks, acting mostly at night wearing white robes and hoods. Their emblem is a burning cross.

The KKK started in the South during the Reconstruction period (1865–1877), gained strength in the 1920s and again during the time of the civil rights movement in the 1960s.

Even today, this racist organization continues to try to prevent racial integration.

Zur Vertiefung der Problematik und Sensibilisierung für die sich anschließende Bearbeitung relevanter Textpassagen machen die Schüler sich Gedanken über das Thema Rassismus, indem sie eine Definition des Begriffes schriftlich fixieren. Dies könnte im kooperativen *placemat*-Verfahren erfolgen. Die Schülerinnen und Schüler erhalten in Vierer-Gruppen ein großes Blatt Papier, das in fünf Schreibbereiche unterteilt ist. Zunächst schreibt jeder Schüler in Einzelarbeit seine eigene Definition in seinen Schreibbereich. Dann wird das Blatt so oft gedreht, bis jeder gelesen hat, was die drei anderen Mitglieder seiner Gruppe geschrieben haben. Die Gruppenmitglieder tauschen ihre Gedanken aus und einigen sich auf eine gemeinsame Definition, die sie in den noch freien Schreibbereich in der Mitte des Blattes eintragen.

Anschließend präsentiert jede Gruppe ihre Ergebnisse und die treffendste Definition wird an der Tafel/auf Folie festgehalten.

> **Racism:**
> a) A belief that race is the primary determinant of human traits and capacities and that racial differences produce an inherent superiority of a particular race.
> b) Prejudice or discrimination based on an individual's race. It can be expressed individually or
> c) through institutional policies or practices.

In der folgenden arbeitsteiligen, aufgabengleichen Gruppenarbeit untersuchen die Schüler Kapitel 12, 15, 16 und 19 im Hinblick auf Aspekte des Rassismus, wie sie sich in Harper Lees Roman manifestieren. Sie finden relevante Textstellen, erläutern sie und ordnen die jeweilige Form des Rassismus einer der drei in der Definition genannten Kategorien (a, b, c) zu.

Die Ergebnisse werden in einer Tabelle auf Folie festgehalten und anschließend so präsentiert, dass möglichst viele Schülerinnen und Schüler aktiv daran beteiligt sind.

Sicher werden die Schüler auch den Gebrauch des Wortes *nigger* als rassistisch empfinden. Der Gebrauch ist in *To Kill a Mockingbird* jedoch nicht eindeutig rassistisch. Deshalb sollte die Lehrperson vorab darüber informieren, dass das Wort in den USA bis zum *Civil Rights Movement* in den 1960er-Jahren von Weißen und Schwarzen neutral benutzt wurde. Erst dann wurde ihm eine negative, beleidigende Bedeutung beigemessen und es wurde durch *Black* oder *African-American* ersetzt. Heute allerdings gehört das Wort *nigger* eindeutig zum rassistischen Sprachgebrauch und ist für Weiße tabu. Im Rahmen von Rap- und Hip-Hop-Musik verwenden viele Schwarze „das N-Wort" (euphemistische Bezeichnung, die heutzutage in den Medien oft gewählt wird) allerdings wieder, um sich selbst zu bezeichnen.

Trotz dieser Hinweise ist festzustellen, dass Harper Lee einerseits Lula und Calpurnia (e.g. p. 158, l. 18, l. 27) und auch Tom Robinson (e.g. p. 261, l. 17) das Wort *nigger* benutzen lässt. Bei allgemeinen Beschreibungen setzt die Autorin meistens *colored people* (e.g. p. 159, l. 6) oder *Negro* (e.g. p. 157, l. 17, 28) ein. (Allerdings auch: „The jail [...] was full of niggers." p. 201, ll. 6–10)

Atticus, Jem, Scout und Dill verwenden *Negroe* oder *black*, während Mr Ewell und Mayella *nigger* verwenden.

Group 1
Find passages in chapter 12 that reveal manifestations of racism. Prepare a chart with the following information:
- Indication of the relevant page(s) and line(s).
- Brief quotation.
- Explanation, comment.

- Classification (a, b or c according to our definition of racism).

Group 2

Find passages in chapter 15 that reveal manifestations of racism. Prepare a chart with the following information:
- Indication of the relevant page(s) and line(s).
- Brief quotation.
- Explanation, comment.
- Classification (a, b or c according to our definition of racism).

Group 3

Find passages in chapter 16 that reveal manifestations of racism. Prepare a chart with the following information:
- Indication of the relevant page(s) and line(s).
- Brief quotation.
- Explanation, comment.
- Classification (a, b or c according to our definition of racism).

Group 4

Find passages in chapter 19 that reveal manifestations of racism. Prepare a chart with the following information:
- Indication of the relevant page(s) and line(s).
- Brief quotation.
- Explanation, comment.
- Classification (a, b or c according to our definition of racism).

Folgende Ergebnisse sind zu erwarten:

Group 1, manifestations of racism in chapter 12:

page, line	quotation	explanation, comment	classification
p. 157, ll. 12–18	"First Purchase African M.E. Church was in the Quarters outside the southern town limits …. Negroes worshipped in it on Sundays …"	Blacks (and Whites) have a church of their own; physical separation, segregation	c
p. 157, ll. 32 f.	"When they saw Jem and me with Calpurnia, the men stepped back and took off their hats; …"	Such respectful behavior, even towards white children, reveals that Blacks have been taught to feel inferior.	a
p. 164, ll. 1–3	"It was customary for field Negroes with tiny children to deposit them in whatever shade there was while their parents worked."	Black fathers and mothers both had to work in the field, but they could not afford a babysitter. Unfair wages.	c
p. 165, l. 16	"'They can't read.'"	Blacks are illiterate; they don't have the same chances.	c
p. 166, ll. 6 f.	"There wasn't a school even when he was a boy.""	Blacks don't get any education. They do not have equal opportunities.	c

Group 2, manifestations of racism in chapter 15:

page, line	quotation	explanation, comment	classi-fication
p. 195, ll. 4 f.	Mr Dean: "'You've got everything to lose from this [trial], Atticus. I mean everything.'"	Mr Dean voices the opinion of the white population of Maycomb. They do not approve of his defending a black person. He will lose clients.	a, b
p. 194, ll. 7 f.	"'I don't look for any trouble, but I can't gua-rantee there won't be any … .'"	The sheriff fears that the white people will want to punish the black defendant even though they don't have any proof of his guilt.	a, b
p. 196, l. 13	"'Ku Klux got after some Catholics some time.'"	If the KKK terrorized Catho-lics, they surely won't hesitate to attack Blacks.	a, b
p. 201, ll. 9 f.	" …, and no stranger would ever suspect that it [the Maycomb jail] was full of niggers."	Injustice, unfair trials?	a, c
p. 202, ll. 14 f.	"'You know what we want', another man said. 'Get aside from the door, Mr Finch.'"	The mob probably wants to lynch Tom. They think he is guilty of the crime simply because he is black.	a, b

Group 3, manifestations of racism in chapter 16:

page, line	quotation	explanation, comment	classi-fication
p. 209, l. 6	"'He [Mr Underwood] despises Negroes, won't have one near him.'"	There are racially prejudiced people in Maycomb.	a, b
p. 214, ll. 14 f.	"In a far corner of the square, the Negroes sat quietly in the sun …"	Blacks are physically separa-ted in this public place.	a, b
p. 214, l. 28	"'Why he [Mr Raymond] sittin' with the colored folks?'"	Dill thinks it is strange for a white person to join black people.	a, b, c
p. 214, l. 33	"'He [Mr Raymond] doesn't look like white trash.'"	Dill has picked up the opinion that if a white man lives with a black woman, he must be considered as inferior.	a
p. 215, l. 19	"'… They're real sad.'" [mixed children]	People are so prejudiced that they won't accept a mixed child.	a
p. 216, ll. 25 f.	"They waited patiently at the doors behind the white families."	White people have the privilege of entering the courthouse first.	a, b, c

page, line	quotation	explanation, comment	classi-fication
p. 219, ll. 18f.	"Four Negroes rose and gave us their front row seats."	Even white children have precedence over black adults.	a, b, c
p. 219, l. 20	"The Colored balcony …"	There is official segregation in the courthouse.	c

Group 4, manifestations of racism in chapter 19:

page, line	quotation	explanation, comment	classi-fication
p. 256, ll. 14ff.	"'I was glad to do it, Mr Ewell didn't seem to help her none, and neither did the chillum, and I knowed she didn't have no nickels to spare.'"	Tom does not speak correct English. He didn't get the chance to go to school.	c
p. 257, l. 9	" … she [Mayella] looked at him [Tom] as if he were dirt beneath her feet."	Even an uneducated, poor, ignorant white girl shows deep contempt for a black person.	b
p. 261, ll. 17f.	"'Mr Finch, if you was a nigger like me, you'd be scared, too.'"	Tom knows that a black defendant cannot count on justice and fairness.	a, c
p. 264, ll. 3f.	"'*You* felt sorry for *her*, you felt *sorry* for her?' Mr Gilmer seemed ready to rise to the ceiling."	White people feel so superior to black people that they consider it a real offense if a black person feels sorry for them.	a, b
p. 265, l. 10	"'No suh, scared I'd hafta face up to what I didn't do.'"	Tom is sure that he will be found guilty just because he is black.	a, c
p. 266, l. 13	Scout: "'Well, Dill, after all he's just a Negro.'"	Even Scout is not free from prejudice. She also considers black people as unequal.	a

In Hausarbeit werden die Gruppenarbeitsergebnisse zusammengefasst.

Summarize the results of your group work in a text that describes the situation of black people in Maycomb in the 1930's.

The situation of black people in Maycomb in the 1930's:
- Official segregation: physical separation of races in public places
- Whites feel superior; make Blacks feel inferior
- Blacks have to treat Whites with respect in any situation
- Blacks are not permitted to mix with white people
- Interracial marriage is unimaginable
- There is no equality of opportunity
- Race is the defining factor in the attitude of the Whites towards Tom Robinson (and Blacks in general)

⇒ Maycomb is a racially prejudiced society in the 1930's

2.3   A child's perspective

Nachdem die Hausaufgabe vorgetragen und besprochen wurde, soll nun die Lynchmob-Szene (Szene 25, 00:58:30 – 01:04:30) des Films näher untersucht werden. In dieser Szene taucht eine Gruppe weißer Männer nachts vor dem Gefängnis auf, um den dort inhaftierten Tom Robinson zu lynchen. Sie fordern den dort Wache schiebenden Atticus auf, ihnen Zutritt zu gewähren. Als dieser sich weigert und die Situation zu eskalieren droht, gelingt es Scout durch ihre kindliche, unschuldige Art, die Männer zum Rückzug zu bewegen.

Die Struktur der kurzen Szene (Dauer ca. eine Minute) entspricht der eines klassischen Dramas (oder einer Kurzgeschichte, etc.) und bildet den ersten Untersuchungsschwerpunkt. Danach werden die filmspezifischen Mittel analysiert, anhand derer der Regisseur die spannungsgeladene Situation übermittelt. Dabei fallen besonders die häufig wechselnden Kameraperspektiven, die nonverbale Kommunikation sowie die Bildkomposition ins Auge.

 Da die Lerngruppe mit dem Aufbau einer traditionellen Kurzgeschichte sicher schon vertraut ist, kann als *pre-viewing activity* die grafische Darstellung an der Tafel als Einstieg zu einem kurzen Unterrichtsgespräch dienen, in dessen Verlauf die Schüler die Fachbegriffe nennen und an den entsprechenden Stellen ergänzen.

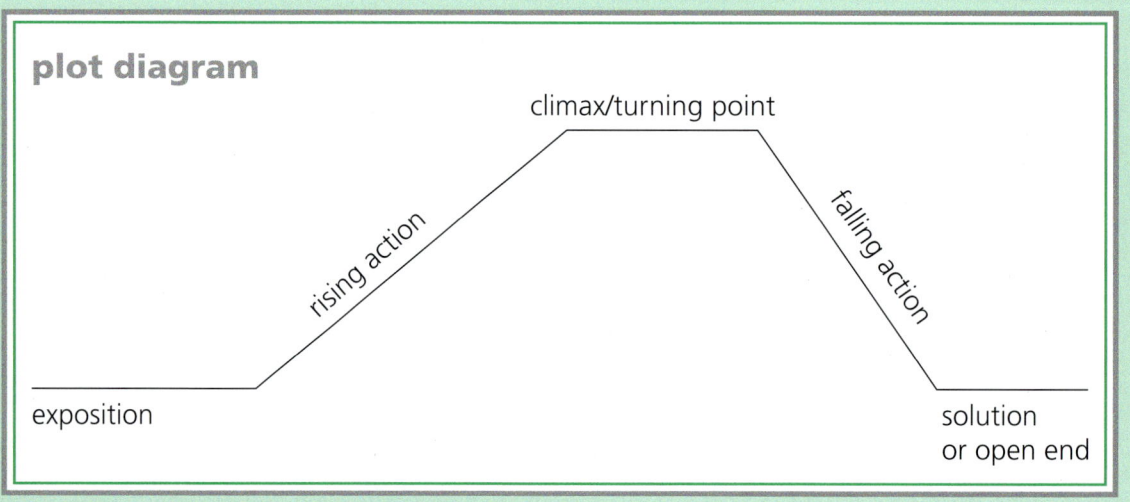

Anschließend wird der Auftrag erteilt, die Szene mit Blick auf den inhaltlichen Aufbau hin anzuschauen *(while-viewing activity):*

> Watch scene 25 (00:58:30 – 01:04:30) of the movie and focus on its structure. Take notes to divide the scene into the different stages of a plot diagram. Use the minutes to indicate the divisions and describe the action briefly.

stage	minutes	action
exposition	00:58:30–00:59:11	We see Jem, Scout and Dill running through a dark and deserted street of Maycomb to watch Atticus sitting in front of the jail's entrance.
rising action	00:59:12–01:00:15	The kids see (from a distance) that Atticus is in no trouble. But just as they are about to leave, they notice cars arriving and decide to stay. Atticus is also alarmed by the armed men approaching him (he seemed to have been waiting for them).

stage	minutes	action
climax	01:00:16–01:01:34	The men, armed with their rifles, tell Atticus to step aside from the door, but he refuses to move. He knows that they want to lynch Tom. The kids find their way through the group of men to stand next to Atticus.
turning point	01:01:35	Scout recognizes Mr Cunningham and starts a polite conversation with him.
falling action	01:03:00–01:03:45	After a moment of hesitation, Mr Cunningham responds to Scout's innocent questions and tells the men to leave. They withdraw slowly. One man keeps looking back at Atticus.
open end	01:03:46–01:04:30	The kids go home; Atticus talks briefly to Tom and then resumes his position on the chair.

Nachdem der inhaltliche Aufbau der Szene geklärt wurde, sollen nun die filmischen Mittel herausgearbeitet werden, die die Spannung dieses „Dramas" erzeugen. Während des erneuten Sehens der Szene fertigen die Schüler eine Liste mit den relevanten Elementen an, deren nonverbale Kommunikation im Anschluss näher analysiert wird.

While watching scene 25 again, make a list of the cinematic devices the director uses to create suspense.

Die Schüler erhalten Gelegenheit, sich mit ihrem Nachbarn auszutauschen, dann werden die Ergebnisse in etwa folgendermaßen an der Tafel gesammelt und in einem Unterrichtsgespräch kommentiert:

Scene 25: cinematic devices used to create suspense
- **setting:** night time, deserted streets
- **lighting:** low key, not everything is fully lit; artificial light on certain things
- **colors:** different shades of black and grey
- **sound:** when the cars arrive, the friendly music stops
- **point of view:** rapidly alternating points of view
- **subtext:** facial expressions, gestures, postures, movements
- **props:** rifles, hats

Im Anschluss wird die Szene nochmals (gegebenenfalls auch noch zweimal) speziell im Hinblick auf die nonverbale Kommunikation *(subtext)* hin angesehen. Um die Schüler nicht zu überfordern, werden sie in vier Gruppen eingeteilt, die sich auf verschiedene Personen konzentrieren sollen.

Group 1
Watch scene 25 again and concentrate on the subtext. How does the viewer know that Jem recognizes the danger of the situation and is determined not to leave?

Group 2
Watch scene 25 again and concentrate on the subtext. How does Scout express her sudden insecurity after saying "Entailments are bad."?

Group 3
Watch scene 25 again and concentrate on the subtext. How does the director show that the problem has not really been solved?

Für die Präsentation der Ergebnisse sollte auch die DVD eingesetzt und von den Schülern an den entsprechenden Stellen angehalten werden, um die Kommentare zu belegen. Möglich wäre auch, die auf *Copy 16* abgebildeten *stills* einzusetzen. Diese können auch zur inhaltlichen Vertiefung genutzt werden, indem die Schüler aufgefordert werden, sich in die Lage der jeweiligen Person zu versetzen und deren Gedanken in diesem Moment in einem kurzen *voice-over text* zur Sprache zu bringen.
Die Ergebnisse können folgendermaßen an der Tafel festgehalten werden:

Group 1:
Jem turns around to look at the group of men when Atticus tells him to go home. He has a worried expression on his face and shakes his head. He then climbs a step towards Atticus and when he says "No, Sir" he looks straight at his father. When Atticus insists on his leaving, Jem moves a step away from him and assumes a very upright position.

Group 2:
When Scout notices that there is something wrong, she stops speaking in mid-sentence and moves her eyes slowly over the crowd of men. She looks up at Atticus and leans into him.

Group 3:
The man in the right-hand corner of the screen keeps looking straight at Atticus. He has his arms crossed in front of his chest and scratches his chin, not taking his eyes off Atticus. He is the last man to turn and walk towards the car and the only one who keeps looking back at Atticus.

Das Ende der Arbeit mit dieser Filmszene bildet die selbstständige Analyse eines *stills (Copy 17)*. Dieses sehr aussagekräftige Bild zeigt den Konflikt zwischen Atticus und dem Lynchmob auf vielfältige Weise und kann in Partner- oder Kleingruppenarbeit analysiert werden. Denkbar ist folgendes Ergebnis:

The still illustrates the conflicting attitudes of Atticus and the men towards Tom Robinson's trial.
Atticus is approached by a homogenous group of men who are not recognizable as individuals. They are wearing hats and the typical clothes of a farmer. They are in the dark and display an aggressive stance towards Atticus. The two men on the left have firmly placed their hands on their hips, leaning forward a little bit. The man on the right is holding a rifle in his hand. It thus becomes obvious that they have not come with good intentions. They represent the dark, racist side of Maycomb.
In contrast to them, Atticus is positioned in the light, almost in the centre of the picture in a slightly elevated place (on the porch). He is dressed in an elegant suit with a tie and a clean, white shirt. He is in a very upright

Stills from the film

Look at the stills from scene 25 and put yourself into the position of Jem (still 1), Scout (still 2) and the man in the right-hand corner (still 3). Write a one-line voice-over text for them that expresses their feelings and thoughts at these moments.

Analysis of a still

Analyse how the director manages to make the viewer see the conflicting attitudes of Atticus and the men at this moment.

position and the viewer can see his face. He is wearing glasses and holding a book in his hand, symbols of intelligence and wisdom. In this way, he represents the hope that racial prejudice and discrimination will be overcome and that justice will be served in Tom Robinson's trial.

Zur schnelleren Orientierung innerhalb des Films befindet sich am Ende dieses *Components* eine Übersicht über den Inhalt und die Dauer der einzelnen Szenen.

Die Hausaufgabe zur nächsten Stunde besteht darin, den letzten Teil des Romans (Kapitel 20–31) zu lesen und die entsprechenden *while-reading assignments (Copies 18* und *19)* zu bearbeiten.

While-reading chapters 20–31

Put the following words from chapters 20 to 31 in the appropriate gaps. You may have to change the form of the verbs.

fraud (p. 268)	to persist (p. 272)	remorse (p. 278)
weary (p. 281)	furtive (p. 293)	
to interfere (p. 295)	sordid (p. 296)	apprehension (p. 307)
pledge (p. 309)	fence (p. 315)	
obituary (p. 322)	to persecute (p. 329)	to acquire (p. 332)
to deny (p. 337)	to leap (p. 343)	
ghoul (p. 344)	inconvenience (p. 350)	appointment (p. 356)
to pester (p. 361)	stubborn (p. 366)	
limelight (p. 370)	amiable (p. 375)	to nudge (p. 376)

1. An _____ is an article in a newspaper about the life of someone who has just died.

2. The smaller animals can easily _____ from tree to tree.

3. The president's wife wanted to stay out of the _____.

4. She _____ with her studies in spite of financial problems.

5. Eisenhower fulfilled his election _____ to end the war in Korea.

6. I woke before the alarm, filled with _____.

7. He's been charged with tax _____.

8. The driver was an _____ young man and so we enjoyed our trip with him.

9. Paul can be as _____ as a mule.

10. She discovered the truth about his _____ past and left him.

11. Throughout the trial, he had shown no _____ for what he had done.

12. Like many celebrities, she complained of being _____ by the press.

13. You should phone his secretary if you want to make an _____.

14. A _____ is a structure made of wood, metal etc. that surrounds a piece of land.

15. Chris kept stealing _____ glances at me.

16. The college _____ a reputation for very high standards.

17. I started to _____ my way to the front of the crowd.

18. A _____ is an evil spirit in stories that takes bodies from graves.

19. He was _____ of the constant battle between them.

20. The men have _____ charges of theft.

21. The kids have been _____ me to buy them new trainers.

22. We apologise for the delay and any _____ caused.

23. My daughter-in-law said that I was _____, but I was only trying to help.

While-reading tasks: Chapters 20–31

Who says that? Add one sentence describing what the characters are thinking when they say this.

Chapter 20

1. Atticus says cheatin' a colored man is ten times worse than cheatin' a white man.

_____

2. In the name of God, believe him.

_____

Chapter 21

3. You think'll acquit him that fast?

_____

4. Miss Jean Louise, stand up. Your father's passin'.

_____

Chapter 22

5. This is their home, sister.

_____

6. You'd be surprised how many of us do.

_____

Chapter 23

7. You couldn't, but they could and did.

_____

8. She's trying to make you a lady.

_____

Chapter 24

9. Oh child, those poor Mrunas.

_____

10. Didn't they try to stop him?

_____

Chapter 25

11. Just fell down in the dirt, like a giant with a big foot just came along and stepped on her.

_____

Chapter 26

12. Jem, how can you hate Hitler so bad an' then turn around and be ugly about folks right at home?

_____

Chapter 27

13. I don't like it, Atticus, I don't like it at all.

_____

Chapter 28

14. You might lose your balance.

_____

15. He's got a bump on the head just like yours, and a broken arm.

_____

Chapter 29

16. Bob Ewell meant business.

_____

Chapter 30

17. I don't live that way.

_____

Chapter 31

18. Atticus, he was real nice.

_____

Übersicht DVD

Szene	Inhalt	Zeit
1	Credits	0:02:30
2	Meeting Scout, Atticus and Mr Cunningham	0:05:10
3	Meeting Jem	0:06:00
4	Meeting Miss Maudie	0:06:50
5	Meeting Dill who is bragging	0:08:30
6	The meanest man, Mr Radley, and his son Boo	0:10:40
7	Mrs Dubose	0:12:40
8	Scout has a talk with Atticus.	0:14:50
9	Jem and Scout talk about their dead mom.	0:15:50
10	Judge Taylor visits Atticus and asks him to defend Tom Robinson, a black man accused of having raped a white girl.	0:17:20
11	The children play at Boo Radley's house and at the courthouse where they witness the hearing.	0:21:30
12	Mr Ewell approaches Atticus in the courthouse.	0:22:40
13	The children go back to the Radleys' house in the evening and see Boo. Jem loses his trousers and has to retrieve them.	0:31:20
14	Scout's first day at school	0:34:10
15	Walter Cunningham comes to dinner and Calpurnia teaches Scout a lesson.	0:37:10
16	Scout hates school.	0:39:40
17	The mad dog episode – the children find out that their father is a very good marksman.	0:42:30
18	The Finches visit Helen Robinson and Bob Ewell scares Jem and Scout in their car.	0:46:30
19	Jem is sitting alone on the front porch, he is getting scared; he finds a medal in a hole in the tree in front of the Radleys' house.	0:49:50
20	Scout has a fight at school because the children speak badly about her father.	0:51:20
21	Scout and Jem find soap figures of themselves in the tree.	0:53:00
22	Jem has saved everything he has found in the tree.	0:55:50
23	Dill is back for the summer.	0:56:20
24	Tom is brought to Maycomb jail by the Sheriff, who is worried about his safety; Atticus goes to the jail and the children follow him.	0:59:00
25	The lynching mob arrives and Scout saves the situation by talking normally to one of the angry men, Mr Cunningham.	1:04:30
26	The trial begins.	1:06:25
27	The Sheriff's testimony	1:08:50
28	Bob Ewells testimony	1:12:30
29	Mayella Ewell's testimony	1:19:20
30	Tom Robinson's testimony	1:27:50

Szene	Inhalt	Zeit
31	Atticus's plea	1:34:00
32	Waiting for the verdict	1:37:00
33	End of trial	1:39:10
34	Miss Maudie talks to Jem who is devastated about the trial's outcome.	1:41:00
35	Tom Robinson is dead.	1:43:30
36	Telling Helen the bad news	1:45:00
37	Bob Ewell spits in Atticus's face.	1:46:30
38	The Halloween pageant	1:47:30
39	Going back home after the pageant	1:52:40
40	Safely at home	1:55:15
41	Finally meeting Boo	1:57:30
42	How did Bob Ewell die?	2:00:10
43	Thank you for my children	2:03:35

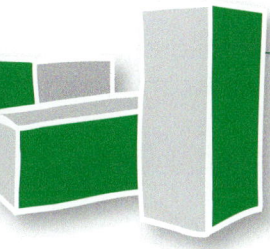

Justice done?

Die von den Schülerinnen und Schülern bearbeiteten Aufgaben auf *Copies 18* und *19* werden im Unterrichtsgespräch besprochen.

Die Vokabelübung auf *Copy 18* hat folgende Lösung:

Lösungen zu Copy 18:

1. obituary
2. leap
3. limelight
4. persisted
5. pledge
6. apprehension
7. fraud
8. amiable
9. stubborn
10. sordid
11. remorse
12. persecuted
13. appointment
14. fence
15. furtive
16. acquired
17. nudge
18. ghoul
19. weary
20. denied
21. pestering
22. inconvenience
23. interfering

Die Aufgaben auf *Copy 19* haben folgende Lösung, wobei die Schülerantworten natürlich variieren können:

1. Scout: Maybe Mr Raymond shares Atticus's opinion as he lives with colored people.
2. Atticus: I can't understand how prejudice can prevent them from seeing what is so obviously right. Why can't they overcome their racial hatred for once?
3. Jem: That would be great, if it really didn't take them long to come to the only possible verdict.
4. Reverend Syke: This is one white man everybody should respect.
5. Atticus: We cannot shield the children from the way people are in their hometown – they must learn to cope with our society.
6. Miss Maudie: Even though the trial went badly for Tom, Jem must realize that not everybody in Maycomb is as stupid as the jury.
7. Atticus: Jem is a good boy. I just hope my educating him will help him to stay unprejudiced. ·
8. Jem: Poor woman – that'll be a tough Job.
9. Mrs Merriweather: I hope I can make them see how much these savages need our help.
10. Aunt Alexandra: Why did they have to kill poor Tom?
11. Dill: It was incredible how the poor woman was hit by the terrible news of her husband's death.
12. Scout: I don't understand grown-ups, they just don't make sense.
13. Aunt Alexandra: I'm so worried. Can't Atticus see that this Bob Ewell is really dangerous?
14. Jem: I wish she'd take off that stupid costume.

15. Dr. Reynolds: I wonder what happened to these kids.
16. Mr Tate: It's incredible – how can a grown man attack children?
17. Atticus: How can Heck believe that I would hush up a crime my son has committed.
18. Scout: It is unbelievable, but Boo is really a nice man and we were scared of him for such a long time.

Die kurze Zusammenfassung des letzten Teils des Romans schließt mit der Frage ab, was der Kurs über das Gerichtsurteil und seine Folgen denkt.

What was your reaction to the court's verdict?
How did you like the novel's ending?

Im Anschluss an dieses Gespräch wird zunächst die Gerichtsrede von Atticus in Kapitel 20 genauer untersucht.

3.1 Atticus – a very special lawyer

Zunächst wird der Kurs in Gruppen von drei bis vier Schülerinnen und Schülern eingeteilt. Die Aufgabenstellung ist für alle Gruppen gleich. Es ist hilfreich für die Besprechung der Ergebnisse, wenn die Kursteilnehmer die Zeilen der Seiten 270–275 durchnummerieren.

Read from page 270 "We looked down again …" till the end of chapter 20. Explain by which means Atticus tries to convince the court of Tom's innocence. Take into consideration his behaviour, the structure of his speech and the rhetoric devices he uses.

Die Ergebnisse der Gruppenarbeit werden im Plenum per Overheadfolie präsentiert. Folgende Aspekte können von den Schülerinnen und Schülern herausgearbeitet werden:

Behaviour	Atticus doesn't behave like a lawyer, he does not use a loud and powerful voice but instead speaks easily and casually strolls up and down in front of the jury. He even takes off his coat, loosens his tie and unbuttons his shirt – for him absolutely unusual behaviour. He does that in order to appear to the members of the jury to be a regular guy, a fellow citizen of Maycomb who is talking some sense to them. (p. 270, l. 28–p. 271, l. 8) However, he is so upset by this case that he actually starts to sweat during his speech (p. 273, ll. 27 ff.)
Structure	**Introduction:** p. 271, ll. 13–19: the case should not even have come to trial because it is absolutely clear that Tom is not guilty. **Main part:** p. 271, ll. 20–27: Tom is not guilty because no crime was committed, however, Mayella is guilty of wrongly accusing him. p. 271, l. 28–p. 272, l. 15: Mayella is described as a woman who'd rather see a man be convicted than admit to a mistake she made herself; therefore, she is not a reliable witness. p. 272, ll. 16–24: Mayella's crime was to kiss a black man. p. 272, l. 25–p. 273, l. 2: As a punishment for that crime, her father beat her up.

	p. 273, ll. 3–31: The Ewells have taken Tom to court on the assumption that a white jury would act in the belief that all black men lie and cannot be believed. p. 273, l. 32–p. 274, l. 27: All men are equal before a jury. **Conclusion:** p. 274, l. 28–p. 275, l. 4: appeal to jury to let Tom go because he is innocent.
Rhetoric devices	There are a number of stylistic devices that can be named, for example: There is the use of **repetitions**, for example of "guilt" and "guilty" (p. 271, ll. 17, 26, 31) to make clear how unreliable the witness of the State is and of "lie" (p. 273, l. 13, l. 17, l. 18, l. 20, l. 24) to stress that it is simply not true that all black people are bad. The **antithesis** of "black and white" is used twice, at first in an almost ironical way when Atticus says that the case is as simple as black and white (p. 271, l. 19) and then again, when he states that some Negro men are not trusted around women – black and white – referring actually to people (p. 273, ll. 21/22). He obviously uses **irony** when describing Bob Ewell as a "God-fearing, persevering, respectable white man" (p. 272, ll. 30f.) trying to show the jury what kind of man one of the most important witnesses of the state is. The use of **anaphora** underlines his urge to stress that you cannot make assumptions about "all Negroes" (p. 273, ll. 13f.), but that there are "some Negroes" (p. 273, ll. 19ff.) who do wrong things, just like that is true of white people. When he refutes the quote that all men are created equal he also emphasizes that "some people" do things better than others (p. 274, ll. 10–16). At the end of his speech, he names Thomas Jefferson and thus uses an **allusion** to history (p. 273, ll. 32ff.). Again the use of **antithesis** at the end of his speech stresses his belief that people should be treated equally in a court, a "pauper the equal of a Rockefeller, the stupid man the equal of an Einstein, and the ignorant man the equal of any college president" (p. 274, ll. 17ff.). In the last sentence of his closing speech, he appeals to the jury members' Christian beliefs by evoking God (p. 275, ll. 3f.)

Die Schülerinnen und Schüler sollen als Hausaufgabe zur nächsten Stunde die Ergebnisse dieser Gruppenarbeit schriftlich zusammenfassen.

> Summarize the results of your group work in a text.

Nach der Besprechung der Hausaufgaben wird dem Kurs die Aufgabe gestellt, abschnittsweise die Rede von Atticus laut zu lesen und mit entsprechender Mimik und Modulation den Text zu unterstützen. Anschließend werden einzelne Schülerinnen und Schüler aufgefordert, vor dem gesamten Kurs eine Textpassage vorzutragen. Im Plenum wird dieser Vortrag dann besprochen.

Nun wird der Filmabschnitt (DVD ab 01:34:00) gemeinsam angeschaut und herausgearbeitet, welche Unterschiede es zur Textvorlage und zu den einzelnen Schülerbeiträgen gibt. Die Ergebnisse dieser Beobachtungsaufgabe werden im Unterrichtsgespräch gesammelt.

- Atticus does not take off his vest.
- The speech is ordered differently:
  p. 271, l. 18 "To begin with …" – "contradicted by the defendant"
  p. 271, l. 25
  p. 272, ll. 26–29
  p. 272, l. 32–p. 273, l. 2
  p. 271, ll. 28–31
  p. 272, ll. 3/4

p. 271, l. 27–p. 272, l. 3
p. 272, ll. 16–24
p. 273, ll. 7–18
p. 271, ll. 26f.
p. 274, ll. 24–30
p. 274, l. 33–p. 275, l. 4
→ Many passages of the speech that we can find in the book are left out in the film version.

- At the end of his speech, Atticus does not mumble, but clearly states: "In the name of God, believe Tom Robinson."

3.2 Reactions in Maycomb after the verdict

Im Folgenden soll herausgearbeitet werden, wie die Bewohner von Maycomb auf das von vornherein feststehende Urteil der Jury reagieren. Die Schülerinnen und Schüler erhalten *Copy 20* und sollen in Partnerarbeit eintragen, wie welche Charaktere auf das Urteil reagieren. Die auf Folie kopierte *Copy* wird auf den OHP gelegt und die Ergebnisse werden von den Kleingruppen eingetragen. Da es vermutlich zu mehr als vier Lösungen kommen wird, sollte auch die Tafel für die Ergebnissicherung genutzt werden.

Mögliche Lösungen zu *Copy 20*:
Jem feels disillusioned and outraged; he cries and is filled with anger and bitterness.
Scout cannot understand the verdict either, but she is not as bitter as Jem.
Atticus agrees with Jem that the verdict is unjust; he is very tired and just wants to go to bed.
Aunt Alexandra is worried about the family's safety; she takes Bob Ewell's threats very seriously.
Dill wants to become a clown because he can only laugh about people.
Miss Maudie knew that Atticus couldn't win but she is proud of the fact that a baby-step towards justice has been taken.
Bob Ewell spits into Atticus's face and threatens him.
The **black people** stand up when Atticus leaves the court house and later bring lots of food to Atticus's house.
The **members of the tea-party** are critical of Atticus because he has defended a black man; at the same time, they worry about the white missionary who wants to help an African tribe. They are unhappy about the way the black people behave in the aftermath of the trial.
Miss Gates, Scout's teacher, stressed the fact that Germany was a dictatorship which was a contrast to the non-prejudiced US. However, as she was leaving the courthouse, Scout overheard her saying that it was time someone taught them (= black people) a lesson.

Im Anschluss an diese Erarbeitung werden die Schülerinnen und Schüler in Zweiergruppen eingeteilt und bekommen die Aufgabe, in einem Rollenspiel ein Interview durchzuführen. Einer der Partner ist ein Reporter einer überregionalen Zeitung, der als Prozessbeobachter nach Maycomb gekommen ist, der andere ist einer der in der Gruppenarbeit genannten Charaktere, der bereitwillig Auskunft über seine Einstellung zu Tom und dem Prozess gibt. Einige dieser Interviews werden anschließend im Plenum vorgetragen und evaluiert.

Reactions in Maycomb

How do the inhabitants react to Tom's trial?
Choose some characters from the novel and describe their reaction in a few words.

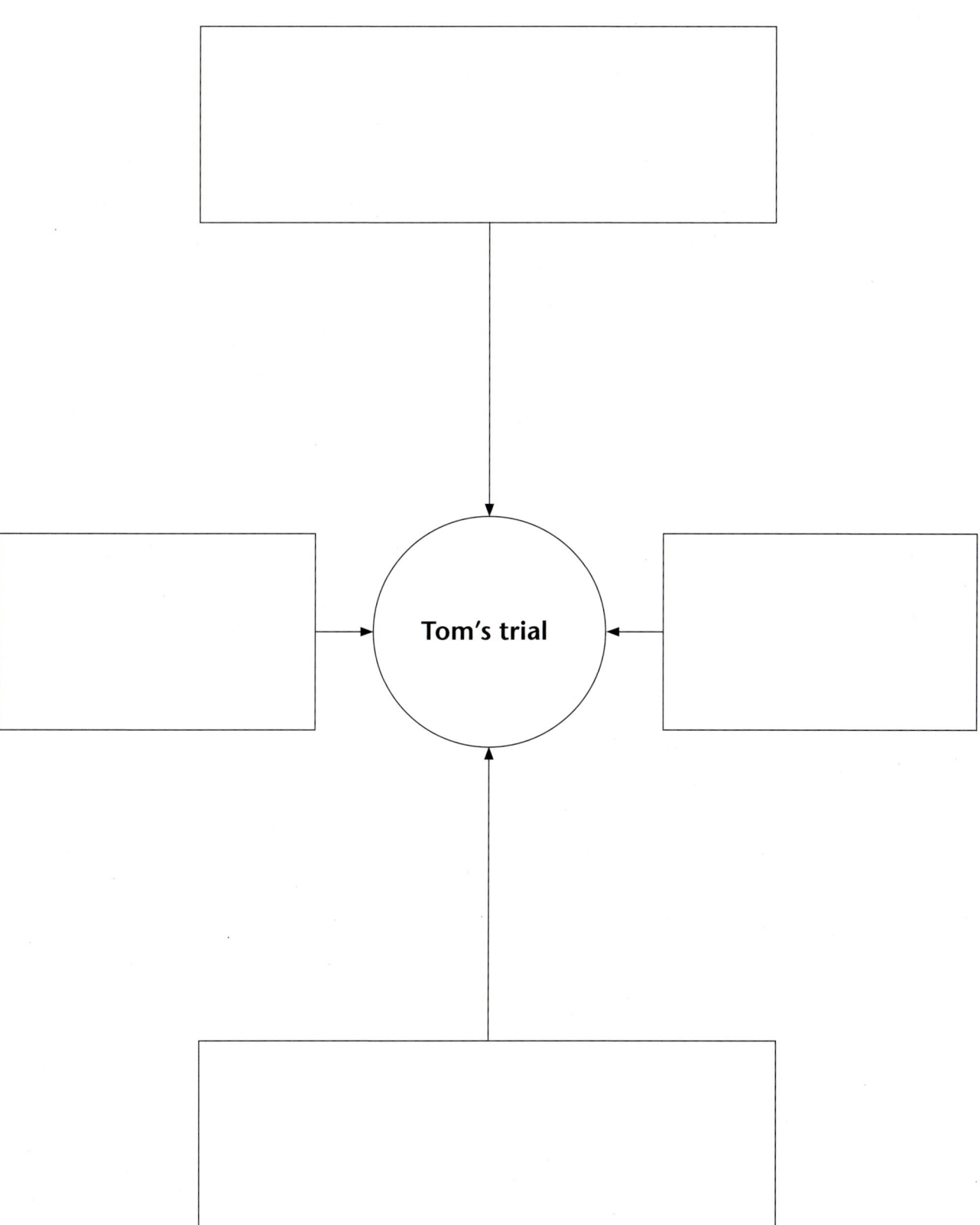

Nach dieser Erarbeitung sollen die Schülerinnen und Schüler als Hausaufgabe die Ereignisse des Gerichtsverfahrens in Form eines Zeitungsberichts zusammenfassen.

You are a reporter for a national newspaper writing a feature story about the Maycomb trial. Make sure that your report answers the important questions who, what, where, when, how.

3.3 Growing up a lady

Als Einstieg in die nächste Stunde wird in einem Unterrichtsgespräch gesammelt, welche Benimmregeln die Schülerinnen und Schüler in ihrer Kindheit gelernt haben.

Think back a couple of years – what rules about good behaviour did you learn as a child?

- be polite
- say thank you, please, good morning …
- avoid fights with your brother/sister
- wash your hands before dinner
- don't talk back
- smile
- …

Im Anschluss an diese Sammlung sollen die Schülerinnen und Schüler in Partnerarbeit Kapitel 24 nochmals gründlich lesen und herausarbeiten, welche Ideale der Erziehung aus dem Gespräch der Ladys abgeleitet werden können. Danach werden die beiden Listen miteinander verglichen.

Now look at Chapter 24 of *To Kill a Mockingbird* and make a list of rules that Scout receives directly or indirectly.

- When attending a tea party, dress nicely (Scout wears her pink Sunday dress, shoes and a petticoat, something which pleases Aunt Stephanie).
- Ladies wear their hats and pastel prints. They are heavily powdered, but they do not wear rouge. Their lipstick and nail polish is only of natural shades. They smell strongly of perfume.
- Aunt Alexandra is worried her emotions might give her away when she re-enters her party because, even in times of turmoil, a southern lady does not show any signs of distress.
- The hostess pours the coffee for her guests herself and you keep passing the cake so that everybody can have as much as they want to.
- Even though guests may utter opinions you do not agree with, as a hostess, you are not to criticize them (but you may be thankful if one of your guests does).

Nach dieser Erarbeitung wird die Hausaufgabe gestellt, bei einem zweiten Lesen dieses Kapitels eine Übersicht darüber zu erstellen, wie unterschiedlich die schwarze Bevölkerung in Afrika und im eigenen Land beurteilt wird.

> **Look again at chapter 24 and work out how differently black people in Africa and in the state of Alabama are viewed.**
>
> On the one hand, the poor black people in Africa need all the support of white people like the saintly J. Grimes Everett that they can get. In this respect, Mrs Merriweather points out that the white ladies of Maycomb stand a hundred percent behind him in support of his efforts to convert the savages to Christianity and to fight sin and squalor over there.
> Back home on the other hand, the ladies are angry about their black servants who a couple of days after the trial refused to work as eagerly as before. They even threaten to fire them. Mrs Merriweather suggests that the church should now support Helen Robinson in bringing up her children in a Christian way, totally ignoring the fact that the Robinsons have never done an un-Christian thing. She even thinks the community should forgive Helen. One of the ladies feels the situation is quite hopeless that the white community will ever succeed in really teaching the black people to be Christians; after all, a white lady is not safe in Maycomb. All of them are aghast at Mrs Roosevelt's visit to Birmingham where she showed her support of the black community. Yankees simply do not understand what it means to live with black people. Mrs Merriweather clearly gives her reasons for a system of apartheid. "Down here we just say you'll live your way and we'll live ours." (p. 313, ll. 21 f.)

Nach der Besprechung dieser Aufgabe wird *Copy 21* gemeinsam gelesen. Die Schülerinnen und Schüler werden feststellen, dass der zweite Teil nicht ganz ernst gemeint ist, aber trotzdem einiges über die Stereotypen der typischen Südstaatenschönheiten verrät. In einem kurzen Unterrichtsgespräch können Gemeinsamkeiten zwischen diesen Texten und Kapitel 24 genannt werden.

Southern Belle

A southern belle (derived from the French belle, 'beautiful') is an archetype for a young woman of the American Old South's antebellum upper class. During the period, Kentuckian Sallie Ward of Louisville was the most noted belle in the South, and her portrait, which hangs in the Speed Museum in Louisville, Kentucky, is often called "The Southern
5 Belle." A Southern Belle epitomized southern hospitality, cultivation of beauty and a flirtatious yet chaste demeanor. The stereotype continues to have a powerful aspirational draw for many people, and books like *We're Just Like You, Only Prettier, The Southern Belle Primer,* and *The Southern Belle Handbook* are plentiful. Other current terms in popular culture related to "southern belles" include *Ya Sisters, GRITS (Girls Raised In The South), Sweet*
10 *Potato Queens,* and *Bulldozers disguised as powder-puffs.*
To detractors, the southern belle stereotype is a symbol of repressed, "corseted" young women nostalgic for a bygone era.

http://en.wikipedia.org/wiki/Southern_belle

antebellum referring to time before Civil War

epitomize to be a perfect example of sth

detractor critic

1. Offer Mint Julep or Iced Tea to everyone who visits your house.

2. Eat grits everyday for breakfast.

3. Refer to your house as "The Plantation" no matter how small your house may be.

4. Refer to all men as "gentlemen caller" or "beaux".

5. Never let a man know you're interested or chase him because you know there are too many men who want **you** for you to expend the extra effort.

6. When you have a dating dilemma and have one gentleman caller over when you are expecting another, claim to be "expired" and excuse yourself for a nap until he leaves.

7. Whenever you are asked to do any work, fan yourself and claim to have the "vapors".

8. Refer to every party you go to, even a kegger at the local university, as a "cotillion". All other parties are yankee garbage.

9. Try to use words like "darlin", "sweet" or "precious" in every sentence.

10. Belong to a country club. If you don't, refer to any club you belong to as a "country club". No one will know the difference.

11. Sit under a magnolia tree with a parasol fanning yourself often. Passers-by will take notice of your belle-ness.

12. Never marry a Yankee unless you want to be a Yankee by association.

13. Never be seen without your makeup and girdle.

http://littlerock.about.com/library/howto/htbelle.htm

grits typical southern corn breakfast

kegger party where beer cans are consumed

girdle Korsett

3.4 Wrapping up

Um die Besprechung des Romans zu einem Abschluss zu bringen, soll zum Schluss das Augenmerk der Schülerinnen und Schüler auf die beiden *minor characters* Bob Ewell und Boo Radley gelenkt werden.

Dafür wird der Kurs in Gruppen von vier Personen eingeteilt, eine Hälfte der Gruppen konzentriert sich auf Boo, die andere auf Bob. Die Aufgabe für alle Gruppen lautet gleich – es sollen fünf Adjektive gewählt werden, die diese beiden Charaktere treffend beschreiben. Als Hilfestellung und um nicht ausschließlich Adjektive wie *nice, crazy, bad* zu sammeln, kann an die Schülerinnen und Schüler *Copy 22* verteilt werden mit der Aufforderung, Adjektive von der Kopiervorlage zu verwenden.

Im Anschluss an die nicht länger als 15 Minuten dauernde Arbeit präsentieren einzelne Gruppen ihre Ergebnisse und begründen ihre Auswahl. Eine Diskussion der Ergebnisse führt zu einer abschließenden Bewertung der beiden Charaktere. Man kann die Übung selbstverständlich auch auf andere Protagonisten des Romans ausweiten und so in einem Rückblick alle Personen noch einmal kurz besprechen.

Als Hausaufgabe wird verlangt, eine der weniger bedeutenden Figuren des Romans in einem kurzen Text zu charakterisieren.

> Pick one of the minor characters of *To Kill a Mockingbird* and write a short text characterizing him or her.

Als abschließende Übung zur Besprechung des Romans bietet sich eine Runde *Touch, turn, talk* an. Dafür wird *Copy 23* kopiert und an den Tabellenlinien entlang werden die Kästchen ausgeschnitten. Die Papierkärtchen werden umgedreht auf das Pult gelegt. Nacheinander treten die Schülerinnen und Schüler nach vorne, nehmen ein Kärtchen, drehen es um und fangen an, über den dort notierten Begriff im Zusammenhang mit dem Roman zu sprechen. Diese Übung aktiviert alle Schülerinnen und Schüler und fasst den Inhalt des Romans auf diese Weise zusammen.

Am Ende dieses *Component* findet sich eine Liste mit *legal terms,* die die Schülerinnen und Schüler als laufende Hausaufgabe während der Lektüre des Romans anfertigen sollten.

Adjectives

Use five of these adjectives to describe your group's character. Be prepared to explain your choice.

open-minded	narrow-minded	prejudice
zealous	modest	enthusiastic
vain	arrogant	snobbish
boastful	outgoing	easy-going
self-confident	dominant	extroverted
introverted	reserved	shy
timid	self-conscious	generous
mean	materialistic	petty
fussy	selfish	ambitious
competitive	hard-working	lazy
demanding	imaginative	sensitive
assertive	determined	indecisive
forgetful	ruthless	vicious
malicious	spiteful	courageous
cowardly	well-mannered	rude
considerate	gentle	affectionate
tender	passionate	smart
naive	down-to-earth	stubborn
likable	tolerant	reliable
dedicated	trustworthy	cautious
reckless	doubtful	respectful
bitter	frightened	condescending
audacious	guarded	indifferent
sad	upset	sarcastic
haughty	mistrustful	solemn
guilty	reflective	childish

Touch, turn, talk

Finch's landing	the Radley Place	Miss Stephanie Crawford
Dill	Calpurnia the cook	"Miss Caroline, he's a Cunningham."
knot-hole in the tree	Scout, Jean Louise Finch	Miss Maudie's flowerbeds
sewed up breeches folded across the fence	the Maycomb County school	Miss Maudie's house on fire
"Do you defend niggers, Atticus?"	air rifles	"You don't understand children much, Uncle Jack."
Atticus with a gun	reading to Mrs Dubose	the treehouse
Climb into Jem's skin	Burris Ewell	Villain
second grade of school	the snowman	a blanket for Scout

Mister Jem	the Quarters	hymn-books
Zeebo	Lula	Reverend Sykes
"Live up to your name."	snake	runaway
Mob	mixed children	the Maycomb County courthouse
black eye	the Ewell's home	Christian English
red geraniums	crippled arm	nickle
black velvet	"All men are created equal."	colored balcony
chicken for breakfast	to spit on sb's face	capital offense

Mr Raymond's sack	Thomas Jefferson	the verdict
the jury	"We're the safest folk in the world."	Walter Cunningham
background	the Mrunas	a tea party
Mrs Roosevelt	"They shot him."	a lady
the ham costume	"She just fell down in the dirt."	democracy
Halloween	"Run, Scout! Run! Run!"	like shooting a mockingbird

Vocabulary legal terms

Lawyer
to read law
to be admitted to the bar
client
to plead guilty to/not guilty to
the practice of criminal law
to bend the law
to be against the law
to serve in the state legislature
to defend
to bail sb out of jail
to begrudge sb a client
law practice
to pick the jury
to know the law
the court appoints sb to defend sb
to expect an objection
opposing council
objection – irrelevant and immaterial
cross-examination
to wreck a case
the state rests
to prosecute
to expunge
defense attorney
to perpetrate fraud
an appeal
the bar

Witness
to be called on to testify
the witness stand
to testify
the witness chair
to identify sb
corroborating evidence
to make a descent from the stand
to dismiss a witness
"The truth, the whole truth, and nothing but the truth, so help me God"
to give testimony
to say sth under oath

Defendant
to be done in by a lawyer's trick
to be indicted on a capital charge
to lose an appeal
to be convicted on circumstantial evidence
the defendant is entitled to
innocent until proven guilty

Judge
to give a postponement
courtroom voice
to move sb to the country jail
legal affairs
to hand sb a subpoena
Chief Justice
to run a court
to throw a case out of court
to bang the gavel
contempt charges
to overrule an objection
a tenet
to go over the evidence
to acquit sb
to commute the sentence

Trial
courthouse
second-degree murder/third-degree murder
alleged
a misdemeanour at law
capital felony
a case comes to trial
court reporter
jury/juryman/jury box
the jury is out
circuit solicitor
the bench
recess
straight acquittal
fair trial
miscarriage of justice
assault

Punishment
to hang sb
jail
to go to the chair
to be on trial for your life
to hear the verdict
to convict sb on evidence
conviction
death penalty
prison camp

Lawmaking
bills to be enacted into laws
the law remains rigid
to obey the law
the Supreme Court of the United States
J.P. court

What else is there to know?

4.1 The Civil Rights Movement

Die Schülerinnen und Schüler sollen in der folgenden Internetrecherche einen Abriss des *Civil Rights Movements* selbstständig erarbeiten und die Ereignisse von *To Kill a Mockingbird* in den historischen Rahmen einordnen. Mithilfe der angegebenen Internetseiten können die Ereignisse entweder von allen Schülerinnen und Schülern gemeinsam oder in arbeitsteiliger Gruppenarbeit herausgefunden werden.
Die entsprechenden Internetseiten sind:
http://en.wikipedia.org/wiki/Civil_rights_movement
http:/www.infoplease.com/spot/civilrightstimeline1.html
http://www.cnn.com/EVENTS/1997/mlk/links.html

> Search the Internet for information about the *Civil Rights Movement* in the USA and list all historical events that seem to be relevant to you. Be prepared to share your results with your classmates.

Im Folgenden findet man eine mögliche *Timeline,* wie der Kurs sie erarbeiten könnte.

Timeline *Civil Rights Movement*

The early years

year	event
1783	Massachusetts outlaws slavery within its borders
1808	Importation of slaves banned; illegal slave trade continues
1820	Eighty-six free blacks sail to Sierra Leone – first immigration of blacks from U.S. to Africa
1831	Nat Turner leads slave rebellion in Virginia; 57 whites killed; U.S. troops kill 100 slaves; Turner caught, tried and hanged
1861	Confederate States of America formed; Civil War begins
1863	President Lincoln issues Emancipation Proclamation freeing "all slaves in areas in rebellion"
1865	Civil War ends
	13th Amendment, abolishing slavery, added to the Constitution
1866	Ku Klux Klan formed in secrecy; disbands 1869–71; resurgence in 1915
1870	15th Amendment barring racial discrimination in voting added to Constitution
1896	Supreme Court approves "separate but equal" segregation doctrine
1906	race riots in Atlanta; 21 dead, city under martial law

year	event
1909	National Congress on Negro convenes, leading to founding of the National Association for the Advancement of Colored People (NAACP)
1923	Oklahoma placed under martial law because of Ku Klux Klan activities
1925	Ku Klux Klan marches on Washington
1943	Riots in Harlem, Detroit

1954 – 1968

year	date	event
1954	May 17	U.S. Supreme Court overturns the doctrine of "separate but equal", ruling that segregation in public schools is impermissible. The NAACP's attorney is Thurgood Marshall, who will later return to the Supreme Court as the nation's first black justice.
1955	August 28	Fourteen-year-old Chicagoan Emmett Till is kidnapped while visiting his family in Mississippi and killed for allegedly whistling at a white woman. Two white men are arrested but acquitted by an all-white jury.
	December 1	NAACP member Rosa Parks is arrested after she had refused to give up her place to a white person on the city bus. The Montgomery Improvement Association, led by Martin Luther King Jr. organizes the Montgomery bus boycott, which lasts for over a year.
1956	December 21	After the U.S. Supreme Court affirms the District Court's decision that segregation on buses is unconstitutional, the Montgomery buses are desegregated.
1957	Jan.- Feb.	Martin Luther King Jr. and some of his co-workers found the Southern Christian Leadership Conference (SCLC), which is instrumental in organizing non-violent protests.
1957	September 25	President Eisenhower sends troops to Little Rock, Arkansas in order to protect and assist nine black students in the desegregation of Little Rock Central High (students become known as "Little Rock Nine")
1960	February 1	Four black North Carolina Agricultural and Technical College students sit down at a food counter of the local Woolworth store. Although they are refused service, they remain sitting there. This triggers a number of similar non-violent protests throughout the South.
1961	May 4	The Congress of Racial Equality (CORE) sends test drivers, called "freedom riders" on bus trips. A mob in Alabama sets the bus on fire.
	October 1	James Meredith becomes the first black student to enrol at the University of Mississippi. Violence and riots surrounding the incident cause President Kennedy to send in 5,000 federal troops.
1963	May	During civil rights protests in Birmingham, the Commissioner of Public Safety uses fire hoses and police dogs on black demonstrators. These images of brutality, which are televised and published widely, are instrumental in gaining sympathy for the civil rights movement around the world.

year	date	event
	June 12	Medgar Evers, Mississippi's NAACP field secretary is murdered. It is not until 30 years later that De La Beckwith is finally convicted for murdering him.
	August 28	About 200,000 people join the March on Washington, where Martin Luther King delivers his famous "I have a dream" speech.
	September 15	Four young girls attending Sunday School are killed when a bomb explodes at a Baptist Church in Birmingham. Riots erupt in the city leading to the deaths of two more black youths.
1964	Summer	During the so-called "Freedom Summer", CORE and the Council of Federated Organizations (COFO) launch a massive effort to register black voters.
	July 2	President Johnson signs the Civil Rights Act of 1964. This Act prohibits discrimination of all kinds based on race, colour, religion or natural origin.
	August 4	The bodies of three young civil-rights workers responsible for registering black voters in Neshoba Country, Mississippi, are found. They had been arrested by the police on speeding charges, released to the Ku Klux Klan after dark and then murdered. The movie *Mississippi Burning* is based on this crime.
1965	February 21	Malcolm X, black nationalist and founder of the Organization of Afro-American Unity is shot dead.
	March 7	On "Bloody Sunday" Blacks are stopped while marching to Montgomery by a police blockade. Five are hospitalized after massive attacks. Earlier in the year, two civil rights workers had been killed.
	August 10	Congress passes the Voting Rights Act of 1965, making it easier for Southern Blacks to register to vote.
1965	Aug. 11–17	Race riots erupt in a black section of Los Angeles
	September 24	Asserting that civil rights laws alone are not enough to remedy discrimination, President Johnson issues Executive Order 11246, which enforces affirmative action for the first time. It requires government contractors to "take affirmative action" toward prospective minority employees in all aspects of hiring and employment.
1966	October	The militant Black Panthers are founded.
1967	June 12	The Supreme Court rules that prohibiting interracial marriage is unconstitutional. Sixteen states that banned interracial marriage are forced to revise their laws.
	July	Major race riots take place in Newark, New Jersey and Detroit.
1968	April 4	Martin Luther King Jr. is shot as he stands on the balcony outside his hotel room. Escaped convict and committed racist James Earl Ray is convicted of the crime.
	April 11	President Johnson signs the Civil Rights Act of 1968 prohibiting discrimination in the sale, rental and financing of housing.

1971 – today

year	date	event
1971	April 20	The Supreme Court upholds busing as a legitimate means for achieving integration. Court-ordered busing plans in cities like Boston and Denver continue until the late 1990s.
1973		Maynard Jackson becomes the first black elected mayor of a major Southern U.S. city (Atlanta).
1979		Shoot-out in Greensboro, Northern Carolina, leaves five anti-Klan protesters dead; 12 Klansmen charged with murder.
1983		Martin Luther King Jr. federal holiday established.
1988	March 22	Overriding President Reagan's veto, Congress passes the Civil Rights Restoration Act, which expands the reach of non-discrimination laws within private institutions receiving federal funds.
1989		L. Douglas Wilder (Virginia) becomes first elected black governor. Army General Colin Powell becomes first Black to serve as chairman of the Joint Chiefs of Staff.
1991		Civil rights museum opens at King assassination site in Memphis.
1992	April 29	The first race riots in decades erupt in south-central Los Angeles after a jury acquits four white police officers for the video-taped beating of African American Rodney King.
2005	June 21	The ringleader of the Mississippi civil rights murders (see Aug. 4, 1964) Edgar Ray Killen, is finally convicted of manslaughter on the 41st anniversary of the crimes.

Die Schülerinnen und Schüler werden erkennen, dass es in den 30er-Jahren des 20. Jahrhunderts, in denen der Roman spielt, keine Aktivitäten der Bürgerrechtsbewegung gab; zu der Zeit existierte keine Organisation, die sich für die Rechte von Schwarzen einsetzte.

 Im Zusammenhang mit dieser historischen Auseinandersetzung bietet sich ein **Schülerreferat** zum Thema *Freedom Summer* an und die Vorstellung des Films *Mississippi Burning* (Alan Parker, 1988), der auf einer wahren Begebenheit beruht: Im Jahr 1964 wurden in Mississippi die drei Bürgerrechtler James E. Chaney, Michael Schwerner und Andrew Goodman durch Ku-Klux-Klan-Mitglieder ermordet. Die Mörder wurden nicht gefasst. Erst 2005 wurde einer der Mörder als 79-Jähriger vor Gericht gestellt und verurteilt.
Folgende Websites bieten den Schülerinnen und Schülern relevante Informationen:
http://www.imdb.com/title/tt0095647/
http:/www.law.umkc.edu/faculty/projects/ftrials/price&bowers/price&bowers.htm

Im Folgenden finden sich zwei Materialien zum Thema Rassismus in den USA der 1930er-Jahre. Beide Materialien eignen sich als Ausgangspunkte für **Facharbeitsthemen**. Es handelt sich um einen Zeitungsartikel zum Prozess gegen die Scottsboro Boys und um den Songtext und zusätzliches Material zu Billie Holidays *Strange Fruit*.

4.2 The Scottsboro Boys

Auf *Copy 24* findet sich ein Zeitungsartikel über die juristischen Vorgänge im Rahmen des *Scottsboro Case.*

In den 1930er-Jahren gab es den Justizfall der sogenannten *Scottsboro Boys* in Scottsboro, Alabama. Neun schwarze Jugendliche im Alter von 12 bis 20 wurden zu Unrecht angeklagt, zwei weiße Frauen vergewaltigt zu haben. Nachdem die Beschuldigten verhaftet worden waren, versammelte sich ein Mob vor dem Gefängnis, um alle zu lynchen, was für die damalige Zeit durchaus üblich war. Im Verlaufe der juristischen Vorgänge gab es insgesamt drei Prozessrunden. In der ersten Prozessrunde wurde über acht der neun Jugendlichen die Todesstrafe verhängt. Es stellte sich jedoch heraus, dass die beiden Klägerinnen vor dem Vorfall als Prostituierte gearbeitet hatten, was ihre Glaubwürdigkeit beeinträchtigte und von den Medien ausgeschlachtet wurde. Daraufhin gab es eine zweite Prozessrunde, in deren Verlauf man feststellte, dass die Jugendlichen keine kompetenten Anwälte bekommen hatten. Der Fall wurde bis zum Supreme Court verhandelt. Am Ende wurde über keinen der Jugendlichen mehr die Todesstrafe verhängt, allerdings über einige von ihnen lange Haftstrafen. Alle hatten mindestens sechs Jahre ohne einen Prozess im Gefängnis verbracht. Der Fall erregte internationale Aufmerksamkeit.

Harper Lee wurde durch diese Vorfälle zum Schreiben ihres Romans *To Kill a Mockingbird* inspiriert.

Lösungen zu Copy 24:

1. Points that make the accusation of rape seem rather implausible/ Aspects of public opinion:
- the prosecution sought to appease both local and foreign opinion (l. 13)
- the case has become a stench in the nostrils of the more literate minority of Alabamans (ll. 15f.)
- one of the witnesses, Ruby Bates, recanted her charges (ll. 40f.)
- the other witness, Victoria Price, became entangled in her own contradictions and offered completely improbable evidence (ll. 51f.)
- prejudices against the behaviour of black men towards white women uttered by the local Circuit Solicitor (l. 44–l. 47)
- juries were very willing at the time to convict any black person (ll. 64f.)
- the concoction of a plan to minimize the penalties for the defendants on a high-ranking judicial level thereby displaying some degree of guilt towards the previously awarded penalties (l. 75– l. 82)

2. Stylistic devies

stylistic device	text	function
alliteration	farcical finale (l. 2)	• to emphasize the outrageous outcome of an unfair trial
enumeration	… one under sentence of death, two … for ninety-nine years. (ll. 4ff.)	• to point out the enormity of the penalties for the defendants

Behind the Scenes at Scottsboro

Alabama justice has yielded to expediency in the Scottsboro case. No other explanation is possible for the farcical finale which left the state in the anomalous position of providing only 50 per cent protection for the "flower of Southern womanhood." Four of the nine Negroes originally arrested on March 25, 1931, for rape still are in prison – one
5 under sentence of death, two for seventy-five years, and one, for some reason inscrutable to all save the members of the jury which convicted him, for ninety-nine years. Four others, with no less evidence against them, have been freed by the state, while the ninth, as though to make things exactly even, was spared a trial on the charge of raping Victoria Price and allowed to plead guilty to assault on a deputy. For that he got a
10 twenty-year sentence in prison, Judge W. W. Callahan explaining that if the rape charge had not been dropped, he would have let him off with fifteen years on the assault charge.

Thus did a self-serving prosecution seek to appease both local and foreign opinion – meaning all opinion outside the borders of Alabama – not that justice might at last be
15 done, but that a case which has become a stench in the nostrils of the more literate minority of Alabamans might be brought to an end. Whether even that objective will be achieved remains to be seen.

The release of four of the defendants, Roy Wright, Olin Montgomery, Eugene Williams, and Willie Roberson, was in no sense the result of a trade or compromise. The state
20 decided what it would do, and informed the defense. The prosecution was tired of prosecuting. It wanted assurances which it did not get, that there would be no more appeals and no more retrials. However, Alabama still holds as hostages five of the nine originally accused – and their sympathizers and lawyers.

It was no accident that Clarence Norris, the first Negro to be tried since Haywood Pat-
25 terson was convicted and sentenced to seventy-five years' imprisonment, drew a death sentence from the hands of the jury which tried him. What better warning could have been delivered to a defense which previously had announced its intention of appealing Patterson's conviction to the highest court in the land? With Norris under sentence of death, the state, anxious to forestall further appeals in the cases that twice have been
30 sent back for retrial by the United States Supreme Court, could afford a generous gesture. It came in the form of a waiver of the death penalty in the trials of Andy Wright and Charlie Weems. In exchange, Samuel Leibowitz waived his right to a special venire of sixty-five required by law in capital cases, and agreed to take his chances on the regular panel or thirty-five. "It was like being asked to swap a turkey for a horse," he said at the
35 time.

One week before the trials ended, the state, represented by Thomas S. Lawson, Assistant Attorney-General, and Melvin C. Hutson, the local Circuit Solicitor, had determined on their course and had their minds made up to drop the indictments against four of the Negroes who were identified with the same degree of positiveness as all the others
40 by Victoria Price, the lone complaining witness remaining since Ruby Bates recanted her charges.

Yet in subsequent trials Mr. Lawson and Mr. Hutson prosecuted Wright and Weems as relentlessly as ever. The mellifluous Melvin, clothed in righteousness and a wrinkled seersucker suit, dwelt at length, in his summation, on racial peculiarities which, he said,
45 made it impossible for any Southern white man to believe that a dozen Negroes "flushed with their victory in a fight with white men" could have resisted the temptation offered by two freight-hopping white girls decked out in overalls.

The measure of their hyprocrisy [sic] lies in the comment one of them made in the interval between the time when the jury in the Weems case retired and the time when
50 it rendered its verdict, which was the signal for the wholesale quashing of indictments against the remaining defendants. Victoria Price, repeating her testimony for the eleventh time before a jury, had become hopelessly entangled in her own contradictions.

expediency a regard for what is strategic or advantageous rather than for what is right or just

inscrutable incapable of being investigated, analyzed, or scrutinized; impenetrable

prosecution the institution and carrying out of legal proceedings against a person

hostage a person held as security for the fulfillment of certain conditions or terms, promises, etc., by another

waiver an intentional relinquishment of some right, interest, or the like
venire a group of people that a jury is chosen from

solicitor an officer in charge of the legal business of a city, town, etc.

mellifluous sweetly or smoothly flowing; sweet-sounding: a mellifluous voice

She had squirmed and wriggled for two hours on the stand, even disputing the steno-
graphic record of her testimony at other trials. So palpably was she lying about some
55 points of her story that Mr. Leibowitz, with the jury excused, asked Judge W. W. Callahan to dismiss the indictment against Weems. At the end of that trial a member of
the prosecution staff remarked that he was glad he never would have to offer her testimony in another trial. "She was the sorriest witness I ever saw in a courtroom," admitted the harassed lawyer.

60 That probably is as near as anyone will ever come to getting an honest explanation
from any Alabama official regarding the reason for the seemingly irrational outcome
of six and a half years of litigation over the lives of the Negroes placed in jeopardy by
a white woman's charge of rape. To those who have been closely associated with the
case from the start, it is apparent, however, that while juries are as willing as ever to
65 convict the Negroes on her story, the repeated defense assaults upon her often-repeat-
ed story have succeeded in shaking the faith of lawyers for the state in the veracity of
the woman on whose honesty the whole case stands or falls. After six and a half years
the high-pitched, screechy voice of Victoria Price has begun to sound a little hollow
and tinny to "Buster" Lawson, whose eyes are on the attorney-generalship of Alabama.

70 If it weren't for that latter fact nine Negroes instead of four might be free today. As long
ago as last December the state made a tacit admission of this fact when the late Lieu-
tenant-Governor Thomas E. Knight, Jr., the special prosecutor in earlier trials, came to
New York with Attorney-General A. A. Carmichael on their own initiative and of their
own volition to propose a face-saving formula to Mr. Leibowitz.

75 At a meeting in the New Yorker Hotel Mr. Leibowitz and Mr. Carmichael agreed that
Patterson's seventy-five-year sentence should be commuted to five years, that four of
the Negroes should get off with five-year sentences if they would plead to charges of
simple assault, and that the remaining four – the same ones who now have been given
their freedom – should go scot-free. Later there was another meeting in the Congres-
80 sional Library in Washington, after which Mr. Carmichael said it wouldn't take him
"more than five minutes to iron out the remaining differences" between himself and
Mr. Leibowitz.

It fell to the lot of Mr. Lawson to report the negotiations to Judge Callahan, who ever
since he entered the cases has been the ablest member of the prosecution staff. Mr.
85 Lawson visited Judge Callahan at Decatur and was angrily informed that the court
never would "agree to accept fifty-dollar fines for rape," which was his method of characterizing the agreement between prosecution and defense.

This apparently was enough for Mr. Carmichael, who without further ado betook himself to North Carolina, while Judge Callahan placed the trials of the Scottsboro Negroes
90 on his calendar for July. The Attorney-General, who by reason of his office is known in
Alabama as "General" Carmichael, did not return within the borders of his state until
the trials ended, and he remained out of reach of influential members of the bar, editors
of powerful Alabama newspapers, and others who sought to make him abide by his
agreement, leaving it to Mr. Lawson, a candidate for the attorney-generalship in the
95 next election, to take the rap for him.

by Morris Shapiro, in: *The Nation,* August 14, 1937, vol. 145, no. 7, p. 170; http://newdeal.feri.org/texts/863.htm

palpable readily or plain-
ly seen, heard, perceived,
etc.; obvious; evident

tacit understood without
being openly expressed;
implied: tacit approval

scot-free completely free
from harm, restraint,
punishment, or obliga-
tion

ado busy activity; bustle;
fuss

1. List some facts that make the accusation of rape against the Scottsboro boys seem
   rather implausible and some aspects of public opinion about the case.

2. Work out the stylistic devices the author uses to illustrate the unfairness and out-
   rageousness of the case.

stylistic device	text	function
personal comment	for some reason inscrutable to all … him (ll. 5 f.)	• to voice the author's dismay at the severity of the penalty
rhetorical question	What better warning could have been … highest court in the land? (ll. 26 ff.)	• to illustrate to the reader how relentlessly the US courts could act when challenged
metaphor	clothed in righteousness (l. 43)	• to make an ironic comment on Melvin's prejudiced proceedings
inversion	So palpably was she lying about some points of her story … (ll. 54 f.)	• to emphasize the implausibility of the witness evidence
personal comment	That probably is as near as anyone will ever come to getting … white woman's charge of rape. (l. 60 – l. 63)	• to express the author's consternation about the hypocrisy involved in the investigation

4.3   A picture and a song: *Strange Fruit*

Der Blues-Song *Strange Fruit,* dessen berühmteste Interpretin 1939 Billie Holiday wurde, klagt die Lynchmorde an Afroamerikanern in den Südstaaten auf beeindruckende Weise an. Er beruht auf dem Gedicht gleichen Titels, das Abel Meeropol, ein jüdischer Lehrer aus der Bronx, 1937 veröffentlichte, um seinem Entsetzen über die Lynchmorde an zwei jungen Schwarzen in Marion, Indiana (1930) Ausdruck zu verleihen. Das Gedicht ist als Reaktion auf das Foto *(Copy 25)* entstanden, das Lawrence Beitler 1930 von den Morden an Thomas Shipp und Abram Smith aufnahm.

Zur Einstimmung auf die Beschäftigung mit *Strange Fruit* wird ein Auszug aus einem Roman von Joyce Carol Oates gelesen *(Copy 25)*, in dem die Ich-Erzählerin beschreibt, wie sie als Jugendliche in den 1960er-Jahren über ihren Vater Max, einen radikal-liberalen Anwalt, von der Aussage dieses Songs erfahren hat.

Es bietet sich an, *Copy 25* auf Folie zu kopieren und zunächst das Bild und die beiden letzten Textzeilen (ab *"an object", l. 13)* abzudecken. Ein Schüler liest den Romanauszug vor und nach der Klärung unbekannter Vokabeln spekulieren die Schüler darüber, was wohl an dem Baum hing, der auf dem Foto zu sehen war. Dann werden die restlichen Zeilen aufgedeckt und die (sicherlich negativen) Vermutungen werden überprüft. Anschließend wird zur Präzisierung das Foto präsentiert und in Partnerarbeit untersucht.

Analyse the picture.
- What does the picture show? State the subject.
- Describe the picture in detail.
- Point out the intention of the photographer in publishing this picture.
- Find a caption for the picture and explain your choice.

Strange Fruit

In the following extract from the novel *Black Girl/White Girl* by Joyce Carol Oates, the I-narrator describes the moment when she finds out what the title of the song *Strange Fruit* means.

My father's favorite music was American jazz, his favorite musicians were exclusively black. I had grown up listening to Louis Armstrong, Count Basie, Duke Ellington, Thelonious Monk, Charlie Mingus (whose piano pieces were haunting to me); there was an old, scratchy record of Billie Holiday's "Strange Fruit" that Max [the narrator's father]
5 played obsessively when he was in a somber mood, in retreat as he called it, from the world of time, heartbreak, betrayal. The voice of Billie Holiday singing this song was haunting to me, riveting. Like Max, I listened to it many times. But I did not understand it: *Southern trees bear strange fruit* … Until one day Max led me into his study, a large, high-ceiling room sparely furnished but cluttered with books and papers, off-limits to
10 Rickie [the narrator's brother] and me, and Veronica [the narrator's mother] as well, and there Max showed me, on the wall, framed, a hideous photograph: a bonfire, a crowd surrounding the fire, a tree with a broad trunk whose leaves were ablaze, and hanging from the tree, an object, a human figure, at which I stared perplexed as a child might stare at a visual puzzle and when at least I realized what it was, I hid my eyes and turned
15 away.

from: Joyce Carol Oates: *Black Girl/White Girl*. London: Harper Collins Publishers Ltd, © 2006 Joyce Carol Oates

The lynching of Thomas Shipp and Abram Smith, Marion, Indiana, August 7, 1930

In einem Unterrichtsgespräch können die Ergebnisse gesammelt werden, indem möglichst viele Schüler ihre Ergebnisse satzweise vortragen. Der jeweils für am geeignetsten gehaltene Satz wird auf Folie notiert und so entsteht ein exemplarischer Text zur Analyse des Fotos, der folgendermaßen aussehen könnte:

> The picture was taken by Lawrence Beitler in Marion, Indiana, in 1930. It shows the lynching of Thomas Shipp and Abram Smith, two black men.
> At first sight, the picture is shocking because it presents two people hanging from a tree and a group of men who are just staring at them.
> In the foreground, the picture shows a group of white men wearing suits and hats. Most of them are looking up at two dead black men who are hanging from a tree. One of the white men is looking into the camera and pointing with his finger at one of the bodies.
> On the right, above the heads of the white men, we can see the trunk of a strong tree and two black men who are hanging from its branches with their heads in a sling. They are wearing rags and their bodies are dangling lifelessly from the tree.
> In the background, the picture is black because it was taken in the night time.
> The picture expresses the indifference the white people of this time showed towards the lynching of black people. The intention of the photographer in publishing this picture was probably to criticize the racist practise of lynching in the 1930's.

Wahrscheinlich wird in diesem Zusammenhang die Frage nach der Anzahl der Opfer von Lynchmorden und der heutigen Situation aufgeworfen werden. Hierzu könnte eine Internetrecherche Auskunft geben (z. B. unter: http://www.strangefruit.org).
Der folgende Auszug aus dieser Website kann aber auch der schnellen Basisinformation dienen:

> "From 1882 to 1998, 4,743 murders by lynching occurred in the US. 3,446 were African Americans (72.7 %)."

Anschließend wird *Copy 26* ausgeteilt.
Am beeindruckendsten wäre es natürlich, den Song von Billie Holiday von einem Tonträger abzuspielen, da so die traurige Stimmung direkt übermittelt wird. Dazu sollte vorab eventuell unbekanntes Vokabular geklärt werden.
Die auffälligsten Merkmale des Songtextes (bzw. des Gedichtes) sind die in deutlichen Worten beschriebenen Kontraste zwischen dem idyllischen Bild der freundlichen amerikanischen Südstaaten und dem Horror der dort begangenen Lynchmorde.

 Die erste Aufgabe von *Copy 26* wird in Einzelarbeit erledigt, da persönliche Eindrücke wiedergegeben werden sollen. Nachdem jeder Schüler drei Adjektive notiert hat, wird reihum jeweils ein Wort vorgelesen, sodass möglichst viele verschiedene Beschreibungen der wahrscheinlich ähnlichen Eindrücke gesammelt werden können.

> **Zu erwartende Adjektive (*Copy 26*, Aufgabe 1.):**
> sad, shocking, depressing, outrageous, overwhelming, confusing, infuriating, upsetting, moving …

Strange Fruit

Southern trees bear a strange fruit,
Blood on the leaves and blood at the root,
Black body swinging in the Southern breeze,
Strange fruit hanging from the poplar trees.

5 Pastoral scene of the gallant South,
The bulging eyes and the twisted mouth,
Scent of magnolia sweet and fresh,
And the sudden smell of burning flesh!

Here is a fruit for the crows to pluck,
10 For the rain to gather, for the wind to suck,
For the sun to rot, for a tree to drop,
Here is a strange and bitter crop.

poplar tree a very tall, straight, thin tree that grows very fast
pastoral typical of the simple peaceful life in the country

"Strange Fruit", M + T: Allan, Lewis; © by Edward B. Marks Music Company;
SVL: Greenhorn Musikverlag GmbH & Co KG

1. Read the lyrics and give your first impression of the song in three adjectives. Explain your choice.

2. Analyse the devices used in this song to express the horror of lynching.

3. Write an e-mail to a friend telling her/him about the song and your reactions to it.

Die zweite Aufgabe kann in Kleingruppen erarbeitet werden, die ihre Ergebnisse in einer Tabelle über Folie etwa folgendermaßen präsentieren:

Lösung zu *Copy 26*, Aufgabe 2.:

Strange Fruit: **Devices used to express the horror of lynching**

text	device	function
strange fruit (l. 1)	metaphor	to make the reader create a picture in his/her mind
blood (l. 2)	repetition	to stress the shock
pastoral; gallant/bulging eyes; twisted mouth (ll. 5 f.)	expressive words; contrast	to give a drastic picture
scent of magnolias/ burning flesh (ll. 7 f.)	contrast	to emphasize the stark contrast between the image of a beautiful, peaceful south and the horror of lynching
a fruit for the crows to pluck (ll. 9 ff.)	metaphor	to show that black life is considered worthless; it does not need protection or care

Weiterführende Materialien

1. Werke über Harper Lee

- Clarke, Gerald: Capote: A biography, Abacus 2006.
- Giddens-White, Byron: History in literature. The story behind Harper Lee's *To Kill a Mockingbird,* Oxford, Heinemann Library, Harcourt Education Ltd 2007
- Hartley, Mary: *To Kill a Mockingbird.* New York, Barron's Educational Series, Inc. 1999.
- Robbins, Mari Lu: A guide for using *To kill a Mockingbird* in the classroom, Westminster, CA: Teacher Created Resources, Inc. 1999.
- Sims, Beth: *To Kill a Mockingbird.* York Notes for GCSE, London, York Press 2007

2. Filme zu „Black America"

- *A Raisin in the Sun.* Daniel Petrie. USA 1961 (based on the play and the screenplay by Lorraine Hansberry).
- *Crooklyn.* Spike Lee. USA 1994.
- *4 little girls.* Spike Lee. 1997.
- *Malcolm X.* Spike Lee. USA 1992.
- *Ruby Bridges.* Euzhan Placy. USA 1998 (TV)
- *Mississippi Burning.* Alan Parker. USA 1988.
- *The untold story of Emmett Luis Till.* Keith Beauchamp. 2005
- *To Kill a Mockingbird.* Robert Mulligan. USA 1962 (based on the novel by Harper Lee).
- *Amistad.* Stephen Spielberg. USA 1997.
- *Do the Right Thing.* Spike Lee. USA 1989.
- *A Time To Kill.* Joel Schumacher. USA 1996 (based on the novel by John Grisham).
- *Crash.* Paul Haggis. USA 2004.
- *The Help.* Tate Taylor. USA 2011.
- *Django Unchained.* Quentin Tarantino. USA 2012.
- *12 Years a Slave.* Steve McQueen. UK/USA 2013.
- *The Butler.* Lee Daniels. USA 2013.

3. Textsammlungen zum Thema „Black America/Racism"

- Flowe, William (Hrsg.): *Goin'down That Road. The African-American Journey,* Cornelsen 1996.
- Flowe, William (Hrsg.): *Goin'down That Road. The African-American Journey* Lehrerheft. Cornelsen 1996.
- Einhoff, Jürgen und Katharina (Hrsg.): *The American South,* Schöningh Verlag 2004.
- Einhoff, Jürgen und Katharina (Hrsg.): *The American South. Teachers' Book,* Schöningh Verlag 2004.
- Edelbrock, Iris: *"Strange Fruit" and Other Songs – Cries for Social Consciousness and Civil Rights,* EinFach Englisch – Unterrichtsmodell, Schöningh Verlag, Paderborn 2009 (mit Audio-CD)

4. Internetadressen zu *To Kill a Mockingbird*

www.gradesaver.com/classicnotes/authors/about_harper_lee.html (Lektürehilfe)
http://www.bookrags.com/notes/tkm/ (Lektürehilfe)
http://www.enotes.com/mockingbird/ (Lektürehilfe)
www.sparknotes.com/lit/mocking/ (Lektürehilfe)
http://www.webenglishteacher.com/lee.html (lesson plans and teaching resources)
http://www.eriding.net/amoore/prose/tokillamockingbird.htm (guide for students and teachers)
http://heliweb.de/telic/baltessa.htm (zum Einsatz des Films im Unterricht)
http://frankwbaker.com (film study guide)

5. Internetadressen zu „Great Depression"

http://newdeal.feri.org
http://newdeal.feri.org/texts/publish/htm
http://www.j-bradford-delong.net/tceh/Slouch_Crash14.html
http://lcweb2.loc.gov/learn/features/timeline/depwwii/newdeal/newdeal.html

6. Organisationen

- National Organization for the Advancement of Colored People (NAACP): www.naacp.org
- Southern Christian Leadership Conference (SCLC): www.sclcnational.org
- Congressional Black Caucus (CBC): www.congressionalblackcaucus.net

7. Musik

- Billie Holiday: *Strange Fruit*. 1939.
- Bob Dylan: *The Death of Emmet Till*. 1962.
- Phil Ochs: *Freedom Riders*. 1962.
- Phil Ochs and Bob Gibson: *Too many martyrs*. 1963

8. Romane

- Beecher-Stowe, Harriet: *Uncle Tom's Cabin*, 1851.
- McMillan, Terry: *Waiting to Exhale*, New York, Pocket Books 1992.
- McCullers, Carson: *The Member of the Wedding*, Penguin Modern Classics, Penguin Books 2006.
- Morrison, Toni: *The Bluest Eye*, New York, Vintage 1999.
- Oates, Joyce Carol: *Black Girl/White Girl*, London, Harper Perennial 2007.
- Selby, Hubert Jr.: *The Willow Tree*, New York, Bloomsbury 1998.
- Twain, Mark: *The Adventures of Huckleberry Finn*, Penguin Books 2006.

Bildquellenverzeichnis
Grafiken S. 3, 60, 61, 62: Victor Prischtt; S. 9: ullstein bild – AP; S. 37 oben: Herbert Hoover Presidential Library and Museum, unten: picture-alliance/akg-images; S. 65: picture-alliance/dpa; S. 73 und 74: UNIVERSAL PICTURES Germany GmbH; S. 103: picture-alliance/IMAGNO/Austrian Archives (S)